Blue Collar and Other Stories

by

Thomas Laird

Copyright © 1994 Thomas Laird. All rights reserved. Contact publisher for reprint rights.

Library of Congress Catalog Card Number: 94-66610

Dan River Press

PO Box 298

Thomaston, Maine 04861

CONTENTS

Detective 1
Diary 9
Freddy The Dancer 19
Virgins 26
The Gulf Of Mexico 34
Gremlin 51
The Edge 59
Album 70
Chronicle 84
Blue Collar 93

8/20/14:

To Omy Belfellow

With warmest regards
and best wishes.
Best –
Tom Faist

DEDICATION

To

Janet, Kathy, Andy, and Anne

and to

Bob Olmsted who persevered.

PATRONS

Pat Jamski
Mary Anne Michelet
Beth Michelet
Jill Michelet
Nancy Suwalski
Mr. & Mrs. Richard Gray
John M. Cummings
Grace Song
Marie & John Taraska
T. Finan
The Book Cellar
Ann Moen
Nancy Bosecker
Tom & Donetta Jenn
Ray LaHood
Sharon Weiss
Katherine Nelson
Mr. & Mrs. Thomas Penn
Gerald P. Maloney
Mike Roberts
Christine M. White
David E. Conner
Lourdes L. Pascual
Dr. & Mrs. Robert Zinser
James E. Johnson

BLUE COLLAR AND OTHER STORIES

Thomas Laird

DETECTIVE

Everybody says Jimmy Parisi's moving up. That's what Doc says. Doc's my partner. Doc Gibson (AKA Harold Michael Gibron, Homicide).

I finally got my shield eight months ago. And what do I do for a living? I walk into some old bum's apartment on the west side, and the old black dude is lying on the floor with his brains splattered against the floor of his curled-up tile in his kitchenette and Doc's telling me that niggers never get killed at reasonable hours. It's 2:30 A.M. Not even halfway through our midnight shift. We don't officially get off until seven in the A.M., but in Homicide you go home when you're done. That was one of the first things Doc taught me: There are no regular hours with this job.

This is the job I've been training for. Training ever since I got out of the Academy, when I was twenty-two. It took me all those ten years to finally figure out I wanted to work in Haggar slacks and Arrow shirts, but I finally got where I am. Finally.

I always knew I wanted into Homicide. It was like a *thing* with me. I've been telling Maryann, my wife, that I thought I wanted to avoid this line of work, but I think we both knew I'd be taking the test to get my shield—it's a gold shield—before I hit my forties and middle age. Somehow Maryann thought my being on the street in a squad car was safer than working plainclothes. But she got used to the new idea, and

1

she almost became excited about it. I suppose you could say she's more or less wary about my new status in the department.

"Why do these fuckin' chuckers gotta get killed right before we take our dinner break? It's always the same shit on this goddam west side...So what do we do now, Officer Parisi?"

I look up from my small note pad, and I see that he's smiling at me.

"I lost my cherry three months ago, on this job. It was the last time we had one of these. So don't yank my fuckin' hose."

"Ooooooh. Belligerence. I adore that in a man."

"I thought the sight of a guy's brains made you sick."

"It ain't the old dude's brains, Jimmy. It's his *cat* that's makin' me about to puke."

I look in the corner where Doc's pointing, and I finally notice a dark ball of something, lying there. And then it's not motionless any more. It's trying to crawl or drag itself out into the light.

We walk over to the mass of bloody fur and see that someone's cut the cat's hind legs off, right about midway up the leg, I make it.

"Come on. Slicin *cats*. Who the fuck we got here? A junkie or a buddy of the Ripper?"

"Whatta we gonna do about it, Doc? We can't just leave it."

The cat tries to howl as he drags himself slowly toward us, but he can't seem to generate anything more than a growl in a low, guttural menacing kind of cat-growl.

"If you think I'm gonna waste a slug on the cat, you're nuts, Jimmy. You call the animal shelter and they'll take care of the goddamn animal. I'm not writing up reports on a discharge because I had to take some fuckin' feline out in the alley and put him out of his misery."

I bend down toward the cat, but as I reach out to him or her, the cat stops skidding across the tile. And then he hisses and spits at me.

"He thinks you came back to really do him, this time."

I turn back to Doc, but instead of him I see the picture, that daytime image that I see at least three times every day. I'll see it when we're stopped on dinner break or when we're walking somewhere on the west side or on the south side or even when we're walking the Loop.

I've been seeing the same slide show since I was eighteen, when I saw it happen.

She's standing at the top of the stairs. Standing behind him. They're fighting, the way they always fought when he came home from the tavern. Only this time I come home just after he does and I see them at it. Usually I only heard them tearing at each other.

Tearing at each other the way this poor damn cat tears his way into the kitchen with his only remaining pair of claws.

But I'm standing at the foot of the stairs, and they're so intent on ripping each other to pieces with their words that they don't even hear me come in. And he's so full of brew that he wouldn't notice if I walked in with the Chicago Bears and had a party in his living room. She's so angry at him that she doesn't want anything but his throat, and she's got her eyes stuck into his face like darts.

"I said I'm not going to take care of this beast. If you want him, Jimmy, he's all yours."

"I'll take care of him...Just give me a minute."

"Well, hurry up before the photographer gets here. I can just see him snapping a quick one of you doing the fucking cat. Makes the *Tribune's* front page, and the anti-cruelty society takes us before the man. Wouldn't that be a lovely way to lose that pretty new shield of yours? You do all that street prep and all that studying to have a cat take it all away?"

"You got a big imagination, Doc."

"Well, you didn't get into Homicide to fuck with kitties, did you?"

"No. I did not."

He smiles at me. He's through teasing because he can see I'm suffering almost as much as the cat is.

"Then why did you join Homicide, Jimmy?"

I have to look up at him because I swear it was Maryann's voice coming out of Doc's lips.

'What did you say?'

"I said, why did you take this fuckin' ass job? You coulda gone to law school and become a downtown fixer. Big money. Nice hours. No midnights. No dead coons on the floors of west side dumps."

Doc is not necessarily a racist. He hates Polacks and Spics and Lugans and Micks. He stole his attitude from *Dirty Harry*, I think. He really hasn't got a prejudiced bone in his frame. It's just his mask for being a hard-ass, a hard soul, they call it. I've seen him bawl, carrying two black girls—one was four and the other six—from the scene of a gang shooting. Both of the girls died and Doc was useless in the field for a month after it happened.

He said, afterward, he didn't give a shit who did it, anymore, after the two girls died on the way to County. He was in the ambulance with them. He wasn't supposed to go with them, of course, but I picked him up at County after it was over, and he was just limp. He wasn't a wiseguy anymore. Just white-faced and limp and dried up.

He asked me that night why I'd joined Homicide. I didn't tell him anything then, just like I can't answer him now.

"We're here to find the bad guy who did this old man, Doc. That's what we're here for."

"Jesus."

I turn and see the cat trying to gnaw at his own stumps.

"Jesus, Jimmy. Do the cat or I'll have to. And you know how I hate fucking paperwork."

I go toward the cat, and he stops chewing on his maimed legs. He is bathed in a pool of his own blood. His blood is mingled with the gore of the old man who was his keeper. The cat hisses weakly at me. He is nearly tapped out. Bled to death, I'm saying.

I see again that same picture of the old man and the old lady. The image is blocking the small remains of this still living feline. It's come on quicker, this second image, than most of my in-brain reruns return to me. Usually the pictures come only once in the morning, one time in the afternoon, and once when the dark comes on.

It got to the point, the last couple years, where I thought I'd have to see the company shrink. You know, the police force's psychiatrist.

But I haven't taken a ball peen hammer to Maryann or Jennifer, our baby girl, so I thought it would go away with time. And mostly I thought the work I do would make it go away when I'd seen enough dying from other people, from strangers, on the job. But it seems my line of work is hardly fucking therapeutic.

They're fighting, I see. Hurling words at each other, and they're at the top of the stairs and the light is behind them so I can't see their faces at all clearly. The fight is always the same: He is drunk and he is late and he has spent forty dollars of his paycheck at the goddam Greek's tavern instead of spending it on the family. And she brings in my name as I'm standing at the foot of those twenty-six steep stairs. She uses my name because she knows it works on him. It invariably makes him feel ashamed which invariably makes him even more furious at her accusations, and then I see her hand shoot out toward his chest—

"Jesus, Jimmy! Take care of the damn thing!"

I can see Doc, now. And once he's clear, I take hold of the cat's scruff. He's too bloodless to put up a fight or to hiss at me now, but he's still alive. He's probably one of those cursed beasts who lives longer than he ought to. His heart keeps going when his body's had too much, I mean.

I take him out of the apartment, at arm's length, so he won't leak red all over my sport coat. It's a brand new navy blue sports coat that Maryann picked out for me.

I take him into the alley. I put him down onto the concrete as gently as I can, but I know I've hurt him simply by moving him at all. He isn't bleeding much any longer because there's just nothing left to come out of him.

But he won't give it up on his own. He's stubborn about staying alive. He's minus half of his mobility. Half of his reason to be a goddamn cat. But he won't give it up.

Another slideshow comes between me and this sawed-up cat on the alley concrete, in front of me.

This time my personal movie's fast forwarded to the part where her hand strikes him square in the chest. She's taken him off guard, I see. They don't hit each other during their brawls. It's usually all words. He's never laid a finger on her in his life, and when he gets really ripped, he brags to his friends at the tavern about his self-control. I heard his boasts when he took me in with him to watch a ballgame on a Saturday afternoon.

He was my old man. He was my father.

She shoved him and he lost his balance and he twisted toward the stairs, suddenly wild-eyed, and then he saw the twenty-six rungs of the steps, and then I looked to my mother, and that same fist she shoved him with now went to her gaping mouth—

"I became a detective to get the bad guys, bud," I tell the dying cat. "And I wind up chasing wino-slashers and weenie-suckers who do their boyfriends with straight razors."

"And now I gotta become the humane society. For you."

I can't shoot him. Makes a racket, and then there's the paperwork

She lets loose with a scream, and she continues the shriek as he stumbles and twists and finally commences his avalanche toward the bottom of the stairs.

I want to call out "Pa!", but I haven't got time to get anything out of my mouth. I want to rush toward the stairs and stop him before he's hit all twenty-six steps.

But it's no use. Before I can move one foot in front of the other I watch my father slam his way down the stairs. But it isn't in slow motion. It is in a blur. It happens so quickly that I don't even have time to suck in a breath of oxygen.

And then her endless shriek splits the near-midnight humidity of that summer's night, and as soon as I'm able to rush to him at the foot of that steep flight, I see he's beyond an ambulance or a doctor. I see by the way his head is cocked that he's broken his neck. I see that my father is dead.

I look up those stairs to find my mother. But she isn't there, anymore. She has retreated to her bedroom as if the fight just simply got itself over with. I race upstairs to console her or to accuse her. I can't decide which. But I have to see her. I have to find out.

Find out what? She shoved him, she pushed him, she caused my father's death.

When I get into her bedroom, I find her at her dressing table, combing her long, chestnut hair in front of the mirror. She won't look at my image, in that mirror. She won't talk to me, she won't cry, she won't touch me or even look in my direction.

The cops came that night and I told them he'd fallen down the stairs, and when they smelled the liquor all over him, they assumed what I wanted them to assume—that it had simply been an accident.

And wasn't that the truth? My mother hadn't meant to break his neck, had she? It was an accident. Nothing premeditated.

That's what murder is all about. You plan it in your mind, in your heart, in your soul. If you've got a soul. And then you figure out the best way to do it. You figure out a way that it'll look like natural causes or like it's been an accident, or like it's as if you, the perpetrator, had nothing to do with any of it.

What were they going to do to tie the old lady in with a crime? Find her fingerprints all over her own house? Would there be a noticeable bruise on the old man's chest?

It was an accident. No doubt about it.

But I still see him with his crooked, snapped neck, and I still don't see my mother rushing down those same stairs in order to rush to his aid.

When the police came, I did all the talking.

"Kitty kitty," I whisper to him, gently.

Then I take him by the back of the neck with both my hands and I yank his head savagely to the right.

He quivers, but only for a moment. His breathing has stopped, I see. I make certain he's dead before I put him in the trash can and put the lid back over the can.

"Kitty kitty," I whisper to the garbage can, before I leave.

I see my mother twice a year. Christmas and Easter. She's only fifty-five. Rumor is she might get married again. But no more cops, she said. No more drunks, she told me last Easter.

My father was a lieutenant in Homicide, too. He was decorated more times than I can count. He was shot three times. Once near fatal.

He fell down the steps fourteen years ago.

It was an accident.

I turn back into the apartment building. I run up the stairs.

The photographer is snapping pictures of the blown-away black man, and the Captain is talking to Doc.

"Forensics'll be here soon, and then we can get the hell out of here...Jimmy...You all right?"

"I'm OK."

"Cat make it to heaven?"

"Sure. He was all through fighting. I just helped him out."

Doc reaches out and lays his meaty right hand on top of my brand new navy blue blazer.

"Always an interesting case in Homicide. Never a dull moment."

"We always get our man. Fuckin' mounties, Doc."

"I already know who shot this ace boon coon."

"You do?"

"Yeah, Captain says a squad picked up a hopper with blood all over his face and shirt about two blocks down the boulevard...Wanna bet?"

"No. Don't want to bet."

"Shit. We catch the bad guys. We find out who did it, and we bring those nasty fellows to justice."

The guys from forensics finally show. Doc greets them, but I don't say anything to them.

"Yeah, Doc. You're right."

I look over at him.

"Homicide...Hell. It's my life."

DIARY

APRIL TENTH
If they think I'm stupid enough to let go of you, they must think I'm too stupid to know how to have this baby.

I'm giving up the baby, but I ain't giving up you.

Rickee--He and me, we went through all that about giving this child up for adoption and he convinced me it's the right thing to do.

Ain't stupid. Just pregnant. And that wasn't the hardest thing I ever did. And giving this child—what do they call it, a *love child*—away won't be near as hard as I thought it would be a little while back.

But my little charm diary—now that's a thing I'm not giving away to nobody. Not to Rickee, not to no doctor. Not to nobody.

This little charm diary, it come with me to the hospital and it's gonna leave with me, too.

APRIL ELEVENTH
It's time. Everybody says it's time. Doctor, nurses, and Rickee, the last time he visited me, three hours ago.

They say I'm dilated enough to make it happen. Doctor says it'll be any minute.

I write all this when the nurse waltzes out of the room to get the man in here to help me start this delivery.

I hid you under my pillow. If they knew what strength it took

to hide you and write in you when they wasn't looking.
Why, they don't know the kind of girl they're—
Big pain, *big*...
Can't write no more. Baby's coming. *Baby's coming*...
God got no pity. God got no pity. God got no—

APRIL FIFTEENTH
Nurse looked in you. Don't know if I want to have nothing to do with you no more. Not private. You been touched. Ain't no charm about you no more. You're—You're common since someone else laid hands on you.
Common.

APRIL TWENTY-SECOND
Can't forget about you. Forgot about the baby girl. Almost forgot.
Didn't see her much. They almost took her out of my arms as soon as she came out. Only a moment, I saw her. A red gooey thing. But my child. My baby. And they cut the cord—that umbrical or whatever—and they took her.
Life ain't kind. Life ain't nothing at all.
Rickee ain't been in the apartment for two days since I came back from County. Says in a note he left me that he got a job in Gary, Indiana. Three day job. It's the first job he's had in four months and it's only for a half week. Says he's gone to make three hundred dollars, and I know how he's gone to make that money, and it ain't from the sweat of his brow, neither.
Rickee steals. From trucks.
There. I wrote it down once.

APRIL TWENTY-FIFTH
Rickee's already bothering me the way he bothered me before he loaded me with that little girl I didn't see for nine months inside my stomach and I didn't hardly see for two minutes outside my belly. He wants to get on top of me and the doctor said that it should be at least six weeks.
And he give me pills and a prescription. Birth control. Says it would keep me from having the same problem. Says a girl my

age—Says my cervix ain't developed right, yet, he says. Says you ought to be twenty something before you go having children.

I tell Rickee what the man says and Rickee slaps me and tells me there's more where that whack came from. He tells me he don't want no girl who takes no pills.

He wants a natural woman, Rickee says.

He brought home one hundred dollars. Says it'll have to do until I can go back to waitressing. I make small money, but we lived on it until I got so big I embarrassed the boss. The customers thought I was gonna come through on top of their tables, and we nearly starved when it was between no work and baby time. Rickee didn't do no jobs while I was big. Sat around and drank some, and smoked some, too. When I told him to quit smoking that funny stuff, he did the usual and told me there was more where that come from.

But Rickee ain't mean, like it sounds in this diary all the time. He's just mean when he's drunk or when he's high. And he can't afford to be drunk and high much cause he don't find many jobs. Even his kind of jobs. They say he's too young. They're afraid to take him along because they think he'll mess up.

Only seventeen.

I'll be seventeen in only about a year and a half.

Can't wait till I'm sixteen so they stop trying to put me back in school. It lasts a few days, school, and then I get myself thrown out on purpose anyway.

Truant man got no pity, neither. He keeps coming around, telling me I've got to do my school until I'm sixteen, at least. I tell him to go to hell, I spit in his face.

He keeps coming back. Got no pity. Won't leave me alone. Keeps asking where my old people are. How the hell do I know?

Got a card last Christmas. Don't know how she knows where I am now. With her boyfriend, somewhere in Washington. The state. Daddy? Shit. Haven't seen him since I was twelve. Momma said he was no big thing and no big loss.

Momma said he was just someone to roll on top of her and then disappear for a few weeks. And then he'd come back and one morning, she said, she'd find that big old weight on top of her. She said she thinks that's what happened the night—the morning—the two of them made me. She used to laugh when she told me that.

But Momma wasn't mean, neither. Life was mean. That's all. And it's life that makes people look so mean. It ain't the other way around.

MAY FOURTEENTH

It's too early, I tell him. It's too soon. But he always gets his way.

He takes my legs, my thighs, from underneath, and he lifts me off this stainy mattress and he shoves his thing into me like he's trying to put a knife to me and I feel something like I'm sticking my toes in a socket, but it ain't no pleasant kind of electricity. It's the burning kind, the kind that makes your hair stand up and the smoke come out of your nose. The burning kind. The hurting kind.

He bangs once, twice, three times. He pulls me off the bed again, up into the air, *up into the air,* and he bangs us both down to the mattress again and again and again.

It's over fast. Thank God for that. At least he made it a fast hurt. Sometimes he made it a slow hurt, before the baby came.

Had to go to County once, before the delivery. Doctor said Rickee almost broke my water. Said we'd better be careful. Said Rickee and me could come up with some criminal thing if we did something to that baby. So Rickee left me alone after that, until now.

It's only five weeks. Doctor said wait six. Rickee says the doctor gets all the pussy he needs at the hospital. Rickee says the doctor don't live in *our* neighborhood. He says that doctor don't know how to count, and he don't know what it's like to go without.

But Rickee's not mean. He loves me. He says it, too. Buys me a Valentine card and a Christmas card. Sometimes he even spends his own money buying things for me. When he's got a job somewhere, I mean. He does. He buys me things. A bottle of perfume, maybe a sweater. I seen the sales slips too, so don't think they come off the back of one of those Gary, Indiana trucks.

Rickee loves me. He put that baby in my stomach and that means love. Children are love. Everybody knows that.

MAY TWENTY-SIXTH

It don't bleed much. It don't hurt much, neither. It's just that I was so tired after coming home from waiting on those tables. On my feet for fourteen hours. Good tips, too. Twenty dollars today. I put the money in the peanut butter jar where he could find it. I wanted him to have it. I can show him how much I love him.

But then he come home with Jackie, and they both are drunk, and he wants Jackie to have a little pussy, and he throws Jackie on top of me—I don't *like* Jackie—and he tells me if I love him I'll let Jackie have a little because Jackie's his partner. And Jackie slaps me when I make out like I'm gonna scream, and then Rickee whacks me in the face twice too, and I decide I'll take what Jackie's going to give me instead of losing another tooth like the time he brought Jackie over here before the baby was three months inside me.

He told me, "What difference does it make, girl? You can only get pregnant once." And when I fought back I got a back tooth knocked out. I told him I'd call the police and Rickee told me he'd throw me out into the street and that I could walk to the Pacific to find my Momma.

So I took it. And I'll take it again.

It's better than walking to find Momma. Way out there in that Pacific Northwest.

Been taking those pills without Rickee knowing it. Ain't going to be like some of these black girls in our neighborhood. Niggers, Rickee calls them. He hates for us to live in a neighborhood with coloreds, but we ain't got a lot of choice about who our neighbors are gonna be.

These pills are going to keep me from being like all the colored girls around here. Big stomachs all the time. They always got a reminder, they say, that someone loves them.

I'm starting to change my mind. The doctor was right. How can I keep my job if I'm too big to bend over the table? Can't. Can't walk around cow-like all my life.

Jackie's rough. Rougher than Rickee.

But he can't hurt me. Those little white pills. They're stronger than his thing. I can't even feel his little white thing inside me no more.

Rickee sits at our dinette table, looking. He likes to look, I think.

So I smile at him while Jackie's still on top of me. I smile at him.

Little white pills, Rickee, I'm thinking. Jackie and you can't ever hurt me again.

He sits up in his chair, and before Jackie can finish, he grabs hold of his partner and throws him to the floor.

JUNE FIRST

Truant officer, again. But this time he says he gives up. Knows I'll be sixteen midway through next year. Says he'll keep on pestering me until I'm sixteen, even though he knows Rickee and me'll be on the move before he can find our next apartment.

Says, "Girl, why don't you let me help you?" And I say, "Help me like Rickee and his partner help me?"

And the man truly blushed. Old man. Must be thirty, and he blushed. I guess he don't want to do what Jackie and Rickee do. He's some college graduate, and I guess his *thing* is too good for the likes of me.

Nobody out there wants to help nobody but themselves. I'm getting smarter as I get older. You damn right I am. Truant officer's a cop without a gun. Goes home at night and watches a color TV. With remote control, I bet.

We got a black and white that Rickee found. It works, sometimes. It's all I've got sometimes, because Rickee ain't home a lot, job or no job.

JUNE TWENTY-SECOND

He's been gone for three weeks and I'm scared. Ain't scared of starving because I got money from my job. Got this place to live--one room and a toilet is what it is—and I'm not going to die.

But where is he? I miss him. Sure he can be bad. He beats me and he brings his partner to me. But he's...mine. Only man I've got. Made our baby, even though someone else has her now.

Gone. Three weeks gone.

I get scared at night. Night's got no pity neither.

JUNE TWENTY-THIRD

Jackie comes to our door and says he wants in. I say no. He slams past me and I make like I'm gonna scream.

"Rickee's in the shithouse," he tells me before I can beller.
"What?" I cry.
"Shut up, girl. Rickee's in County. He fucked up."
That's all he tells me. Nothing clear. But his mind's on something other than what it usually is when he's around here, so I don't go looking to upset him.
"Don't want no pussy from you, girl. You're dirty. Probably got them AIDS. Only fucked you when I was drunk."
I swing at him with my fist, but he laughs and ducks all at once and he slams the door in my face.
When he goes, I sit in front of our black and white. Then I turn it on.
Pictures of the world on the six o'clock news. Dan Rather. Handsome man. Too old. Way too old for me.

JULY SEVENTEENTH

Rickee never called. He's going to Joliet, I read in the papers. Five years. Theft. Felony. Seventeen, and he's an adult. Carried a weapon, stuck a night watchman. Night watchman was O.K. That's why Rickee didn't get more.

When Rickee gets out, maybe four years, with probation, I'll be almost twenty. Old lady then. Start to get gray. Ha ha. Very funny. Old woman.

Nah. Stick to my pills. Stay away from Jackie. Move out of this apartment before he gets drunk and comes back for what he craves when he's drunk. Rickee's partner. Share and share alike. When I take those pills I can shrivel his little white thing up inside me. I know how, now.

I can be mean too. I can learn. Don't need school. I'm smart. Don't need algebra to stay away from Rickees and Jackies. Just need my little pills and my two fast feet.

JULY TWENTIETH

Jackie comes back. Drunk. Pushes past the door. Tries to take my peanut butter jar. Knows where we put our money because Rickee told him everything. Partners.

"Get your things off, ugly little girl," he says.

I tell him I'll scream this time. Get the cops here. He'll join

Rickee in Joliet for rape this time. No more jumping on top of me, I yell at him.

He laughs and comes for me. I back up to our kitchen sink, and a cockroach scoots across my fingers and I scream. Jackie jumps back when I beller, and when he jumps, I turn and find the glass peanut butter jar. I grab hold of it, and before I can think, I fling it in Jackie's face.

He don't go down, but a big piece of glass sticks between his eyes. He takes it out with his right hand, and then the blood spurts so quick I think I'll be sick.

But I don't get sick. Jackie gets sick. On his knees, blood and sick coming out of him. And then he faints, straight-away, face-first onto our tile floor. I feel his neck, like I seen in the soap shows when the doctor checks an accident victim, you know, and I feel a strong pulse. Jackie ain't dead, and ain't gonna die. Not here. Not today. Rickee is doing just fine with his boyfriends in Joliet too, I bet. I read about prisons.

But I can't wait for Jackie to wake up. I'll call County and have them clean this piece of shit up.

That's right. Piece of shit.

No more Jackie, coming in drunk, flopping on top of me while his partner gets a good view. His partner, in prison.

I laugh inside when I think of Rickee.

"You're where you were headed, lover."

I laugh and laugh, inside. Over and over, until my sides hurt. The laughter wants to come out, but I'm afraid with Jackie on my floor, full of sick and blood.

Got to get out.

Close my eyes and reach into the mess for the thirty-five dollars that was in my peanut butter jar. Floor feels sticky. Stinks. Almost makes me sick.

But I find the bills, I take them to the sink and I put a little water on them. Clean them off. The sick and the blood. Jackie is quiet, but the bleeding's stopped all by itself.

He'll be a man and awake in a minute.

Time to be gone. Now. Get out get out get out get out get out get out

JULY THIRTY-FIRST
End of summer coming very soon. I can smell it. Always could, even when I was living with Momma.

I moved in with Julie, another waitress. Just temporarily, I told her. She has a boy friend too, but he don't come looking to flop on anyone but Julie. They are in love. The way I used to think it was for Rickee and me.

But I learn. I'm not stupid. I learn things.

Jackie comes by the restaurant, the diner, and tries to threaten me because I bust his head, but Julie and the owner, Sal, tell Jackie to get the fuck out. That's just what they said. And Jackie is convinced that Sal means to use his cleaver, so Jackie gets the fuck out. I laughed and Julie laughed, and Julie hugged me and we laughed some more.

But I can't stay with Julie because she's got her Donald and she don't need me in her way. Don't want her to wind up no old maid because of me—and she's already nineteen.

So I find out Momma's phone number, in Washington.

How do I find out? Truant officer, that's how. He says he wants to help me, so I say, O.K., help me. Find out where my Momma is. He warns me that she might not want to help me, but I tell him she's the only chance I got. Got to depend on Momma for pity, I tell the truant officer.

God got no pity, I tell him.

AUGUST THIRTY-FIRST
Momma sends busfare. Her boyfriend told her she couldn't just say no. He told her that at least she ought to give me a chance to see if I could live with them in Seattle. I don't know how sure Momma is about me coming out there. All this is is a bus ticket and a vacation, she says, and then we'll play it by ear. Her boyfriend wants her to do the right thing, she says. His ex-wife beat up their two kids. One of them died and the ex-wife went to jail for a long time. County took the other kid away, and Momma's boyfriend spent three months in the alcoholics' tank, drying up.

Momma says he's a good man. A logger. First good man she ever wound up with. He won't try any slick stuff with me, she says. He wants a daughter, she says. Lost one already, and don't want to lose anybody else.

I like bus rides. Long and quiet. Can put my little charm diary on my lap and write and write and write.

I don't think about Rickee much and I think about that bastard Jackie even less. I'm going to write real letters to Julie and Sal to let them know what happens with Momma and her new boyfriend.

Ain't going to get my hopes up too high. Don't expect any pity. Don't want any.

It was cold, on the way out of the Loop. Like November in August. The trees'll be turning soon. I look for them to do it every year, and they do.

It'll be my birthday in a few more months. Wintertime.

Sweet sixteen.

I'm laughing inside.

Sweet sixteen, and never been kissed.

FREDDY THE DANCER

Freddy the Dancer. Me. The world's greatest living softball pitcher. I take that sixteen inch Windy City Clincher. I place both feet on the pitching rubber. I wind up step off come from under the side of the knee with that right hand and make it look like sure here it comes here it comes but the ball slides back down into my palm trapped. Fake number one. Next time it's a step off the rubber two flickering motions with the wrist and the palm and again. Fake number two. This is the last one, he with the bat, he knows it—here it comes. It flies, it's winging, it's shuddering at the top of its flight. It's gleaming reaming streaming white and the laces and the print I see them spinning twisting downward. God help you, pal. Freddy the Dancer has struck again.

It floats. It's suspended. Not slow motion. It merely stands and waits and I can see his eyes widening the bat hitches back the muscles in his thighs and calves tighten and his forearms are tightening his release is building. Like watching an accident (in traffic) about to happen. Inevitable. He's gonna murder that ball. All that faking all that form gonna be for nothing. Dance Freddy dance. There's no music. I have no partner. On the way to the plate. God help her. 'Her' is for ships. This is a Windy City Clincher. Not human. Justaballball-game. God help me, he's going to right. Big gaping hole. He's shifting toward right. Left foot toward the first base line. Right foot skips to his left in the batter's box. His eyes and head are down on the ball. Just like Alston says in his book. He's out to advance the runner by going to the right side. He's a hitter. God help me.

I can remember back in high school when I had such a bad time making the baseball team. I always tried out for the wrong position. I tried out for pitcher my freshman year. I hit three consecutive batters in a pre-season game and never made the frosh team. I tried the same thing the next year and hit four batters in the first pre-season game. I didn't play a great deal of baseball until my junior and senior years, when I moved to center field. In center field I was too far away from the players to hurt anybody with my throws. Hitting gradually became one of my strengths, too.

But. I was always a better softball player than a hardball player. Games which weren't varsity sports, I was tough in them all. I could never conquer sports that were popular, or important.

Softball is played mostly in the summer. Not in the spring or fall. It's a hot weather sport. You can smell a softball game. You can see stained jerseys with *Alphonso's 33rd Street Tap* on the back side or *Garvey's Come Back Inn* lettered across the shoulder blades. Big time players don't wear hats. They never wear baseball gloves. No gloves means lots of bandaged fingers and thumbs.

I'm good at softball because it's a meaningless frustrated jock's attempt at a second childhood. Cynical description? I guess. Yeah, I was jealous of the guys who made it big. The guys who got a free ride to Illinois or Michigan or O.S.U., or even to a junior college. But I could never come to hate them because most of them were my friends.

They were the ones who were really big with the *Cheeses*. You know, the broads who were the social queens of the high school or the college. They were the guys who were voted most likely to succeed, most likely to kiss ass, most likely to wind up with brown on their snout. I always pretended to hate the Cheeses or the Susie Sororities, but I always admired them secretly and felt like hot shit if one of them paid attention to me.

But they never paid much attention to me because softball games don't attract big crowds. Just wives and steadies and other meaningless frustrated jocks.

I think if I ever understand this game I'll understand a big chunk of myself. I like to think of myself as a superior type with a superior cynical overview of a cruel and uncaring world, but then I sound like a Lit course that reads words and sentences but doesn't get the meaning of the story. In other words, I see Smokey the Bear, but I missed the rest of his forest; you know, his real reason for being?

It'd be fun to be that fast half back who scores the winning touchdown and Frank and Howard and Whoever all lavish the praise while U.P.I. and A.P. are all snapping pictures and I hear the clicking and the roaring and I see the flash of bulbs faceless mouths and palms yelling and clapping me across the white goal stripe...I had a beer bottle thrown at me once for missing a throw to second base. It was a game against *Jake's Pit Stop.*

I always wanted to marry the captain of the cheerleading squad, even though in public I had been quoted as saying that cheerleaders only shit in flavors of pistaccio and chocolate chip. When they pissed I could imagine the water in the bowl would part in its middle, almost religiously.

Which is why I almost always wound up with seconds. If two of us were working on a rap with two birdies, I'd get the Avis. I've been thrown out at second base on apparent hits to the outfield, too.

However, ahem, I don't think of myself as a loser. As I say, I can dance on that goddam mound. The problem is that they don't offer softball players five year, no cut, hundred grand contracts. Maybe a pizza at 'Louie's' for half price for the season's first grand slammer.

So what do I do for a living? I have a job. A very nondescript job. I work with people, I make twelve grand a year, I own a 1971 Pontiac Bonneville, I rent a house in a southwestern suburb, I bowl on Thursdays in the fall, I have one heavy romance going on at the moment, and I actually give a shit who wins the Bear games.

About that one heavy romance. Unfortunately that 'heavy' bit is just that, lately. She's been bitching about everything I do. I say the wrong things at the wrong times, I make too much noise chewing gum, I don't answer questions 'just as they're asked' about insignificant details (the time I'll pick her up, where we're going, what movie we're seeing, et al). She got pissed off once because I didn't check all the departure times for a bus she was going to take on a short visit up north.

She's constantly bitching about our sex life. Not that it's too infrequent. Again, little things. I don't manicure my fingernails and she says it's painful during foreplay. I don't shave closely enough and the resulting friction is the cause for her bumper crop of blackheads. And, I don't believe in rubbers, (she doesn't believe in the pill or the crazy foam) so we have to live through coitus interruptus.

I'm different with her. Heard that before? On the mound I've got confidence. I know what I can do. But with her, I'm constantly in fear of screwing up. I create my own nightmares about little things I'll do to piss her off. I'm afraid she won't love me, she will love me, she won't fuck me.

What if she kisses me off? I'm afraid that I won't be understood as well, I won't get tickled as well (she's one great tickler. Tickling involves a great deal of technique and proper usage of the tips of the fingernails). All this, I know, is leading to the fact that she'll soon hate me because she'll soon know how insecure I am. Great. I need her because I'm insecure and I'll lose her for the same. Bitch. Son of.

I wrote poetry for her. The only poetry that wasn't born out of total disgust for everything. The only poetry that wasn't putrid and sour from me was unsheathed from her loins (and mine). I was musical, lyrical with her.

I remember once we decided to do what all good Christians refuse to do, as long as there's more than one person doing it at a time. We decided to baptize each other in the shower at a motel. I remember I made sure not to get her hair wet. It was long and brown and curly. I remember the wet and the soap and the steamy warm. I remember, also, making it standing up against the cold tiled wall. We stopped, after a while, dried off, and later continued and finished on the bedspread. I wanted to stuff her with offspring. I told her so. When I came, though, it was on her belly. Come is not one of my favorites to look at, but I looked at it and I studied it. The usual accompanying pains pressed on for a long time that night.

Blue balls is what it's called. Incomplete intercourse. When she sees my face twisted up she immediately goes into a routine about, "How do you think I feel?" However, I never get the impression she has any trouble pissing when we get through with all that.

Our second baseman ain't a tower of grace. He doesn't move

well to his right or to his left. I've got to cover territory for him. Christ, I cover first for him on just about any ball that's not a line shot right at him. He keeps saying he's got real quick wrists, though. The fat bastard is out of his element. He's begun his lifetime slump. However, he is the Captain and one of the founding fathers. Half his goddam paycheck goes to Augie Busch and his brew and the other half goes to Windy City and the Louisville Slugger bat company.

Like a drowning man. All before my eyes. It's dancing now. Not me. Those biceps of his are bulging and the veins in his neck are almost blown out of the flesh. The Clincher makes it down to his letters and he connects. I mean it's solid. The meat. The whole shitload. But the bastard skips his back foot back in the batter's box where it started, his left foot is staring at me, about groin level, and he swings so hard that I can hear something heavy and guttural spit at me as if the bat was doing the grunting. The son of a bitch has keyholed me. Lined one right off my kneecap. All the neon signs across the street become larger and redder—Tweeeeee!!!!! I'm screaming, my knee is screaming. Big big red. Bull, cape, matador. My leg throbs. Gimme a surgeon. Drowning. The season flies by. The seasons are all flying by. I'm gone. I know it. And so does that big bastard on first base. Grinning. Teeth. Nice, white, even. Grinning. Bastard.

I'm a young man. I got a sex life, I'm an athlete. I'm in one piece. I got nothing to worry about.

She isn't going to leave me just yet and if she does there are others who like crummy fingernails and steel woolly faces and—

My old man is funny. Not funny strange, but funny humorous. I remember the time I gave him the whole story about catching the clap from some 200 pound go-go dancer type in Oshkosh. He wasn't concerned. He laughed at me and asked me if I was spotting up my underwear. I said no and he said nothing more about it. Just laughed one more time.

My old man is a fantastic reader. He can absorb books by the legion, by the ton. He can retain everything he's read. He doesn't have a four-year diploma from college. And that is why my old man and I are making twelve grand. He wants to retire in California. California, the goddam fruitcake capital. I tell him it's expensive, it's distant, it's too much for an old man and his old woman, but he tells me, "wanna die there." What an earthy thought, huh? I bought the old man a copy of *The Grapes Of Wrath* for his birthday. I keep asking him if he's read it, and he keeps saying he doesn't like to read at night because he's got to read all day long.

I only saw him cry once. It sure as hell didn't seem dramatic at the time because he kind of choked and blurted something out in anger at me about getting my ass out of school in less than six years and something like "can't take this any more" and I looked at him just like I was waiting for a punch line and nothing happened and I started apologizing for me being an asshole (he got mad at that reference, too) and I kept babbling, "It'll be all right, it'll be all right."

My old man's old man was a pretty big time doctor. General practitioner. Opened an industrial medical center thing. Roses, huh? Grandad died when the old man was fourteen. My old man was fourteen right at the beginning of the goddam Depression. My old man works in a paint factory and schedules rednecks enough overtime for them (the rednecks) to take Hawaiian vacations every year. My old man's biggie came when he made it to Tampa, Florida, by jet. By coach, of course.

I remember him arguing with an uncle about the A-Bomb and the H-Bomb and about fallout and all that. The uncle claimed that he didn't want to live even if the bomb didn't get him and his kids and wife. My old man sat cold and quiet and told him that all he wanted was for his kid to live forever. The old drizzily shit didn't know I was anywhere in the room.

The man's got cancer, somewhere in his body, and they're treating it with cobalt. He feels shitty, generally, and I heard from the old lady that he's talking insurance and coverage and all that to her. The specialist tells him the cobalt's working. My old man, I can picture it, smiles at the doctor, pays the nurse, and mumbles, "Lying sack of shit" under his breath as he walks out the clinic door.

I remember zero about the hospital and the bandages and the ice and the crutches. They told me to stay off it for a couple of weeks. For a couple of weeks. In a couple of weeks it'll be September. It's all over. No playoffs, no stag down at the K.C., no nothing. It's over, simple as that.

Two beers and I'm pissing and moaning to old man Garvey behind the bar. But this time when I walk in with those crutches and that light tan wraparound knee bandage I'm not out looking for sympathy. From Garvey or my broad or from that fat ass second baseman.

I'd like to get that grinning keyholing even toothed bastard. I'd like to see his head on a platter with a Clincher stuffed between those teeth. I'd like to sit like a king at the head of a huge table and dress Garvey in a jester's costume, shove my old man to my right hand side, see that fat second baseman waiting on my table filling up water glasses while naked nubile big titted Ohio State Cheerleaders slobber at the crust and crumbs I leave for my hounds. Then I'd retire to my chambers and she'd come in in one of those Elizabethan dresses that'd stuff her medium sized boobs into a fantastic snapshot of cleavage. I'd ravish her with my fingernails scratching and my bubblegum popping. When it was over I'd do it again to her. Just one more time, to get it right.

The Cubs are in last place. They might move the Sox to Seattle. I'm a Sox fan. The Sox are in 5th (next to last). The Cubs are always on Garvey's tube. The son of a bitch. He knows we're (I'm) Sox fans. Nobody's noticed these goddam crutches. Tough. That doesn't make any difference because in this stinky smelly lazy fat man's game there's always another season. Freddy'll dance again, and again. Next time. I'll get those feet back on the ground and I'll throw the fake and another and I'll leave that toothy bastard's jock in the batter's box. I'll rhumba, watusi, and bump all over him. I can hear the music now. I don't need a juker. I can hear that music now.

VIRGINS

It was hopeless. We were another six or seven hours away from Chicago, and it was hopeless.

"What's one more parade? Who needs it?"

The Orphan is becoming stiff. I can always tell when he's ready to go under. I could always tell when he had snooted too much even back when we were in-county.

"Take it easy, James. If we leave right now, we could make it in time to see Westy on the ten o'clock news in Chicago."

"We could see Westy right here on the ten o'clock news. On my black and white portable. I carry it everywhere, you noble savage, you redman, you."

"James, my man, the only way we're going to make that parade is if you're sober enough to help me drive through, at 80 miles per hour. If we don't get busted by the state bears along the highway."

"What's one more parade, Indian?"

"We never had no parades, as I recall."

We're stopped at one of these interstate rest stops. I'm not sure if we're in South Dakota or Iowa, we're so close to the border of the Hawkeye state. We've got several hundred miles left to travel to catch the big Vietnam Veteran's Parade in downtown Chi. And I don't think we're going to make it, the shape we're in.

"There'll be guys with legs and guys with no legs. How's that for variety? You think Hanoi Jane'll make it?" he asks.

"You better slow down."

James Hugh Marten is a very handsome Orphan. He is also starting to do what so many forty year old men do. Gray around the sideburns. It only makes him more attractive to females, his wife Cee told me before he left San Francisco, their hometown. She called me long distance when he left for our place in Montana. It's in a place called Lupus. I left our ranch in the hands of my crazy old man, Marvin, and in the hands of my not-so-crazy second wife, Cathy. She'll have to handle the old goat because no one else has ever been able to.

He's calmed down since our second son was born, last spring, however.

And Orphan has two of his own; a teenaged son and a a three year old filly who was a surprise child to them both. He's a lawyer in Frisco and she's an M.D. there. They thought their careers couldn't tolerate another baby, but nature showed them who's boss.

That's the way it's always worked out in my life, too. Nature needs no body counts to let it be known it's the enforcer.

So James picks me up in his red van—where were these vehicles when we needed them back in high school in the sixties—and we start traveling south and east to get to The City With The Big Shoulders. I've never been to Chi, but the Orphan has.

It's the Big Payback, this parade, we've told each other. See, all those movies and books did some good afterall. They finally made our war look good to a lot of people. That's the sad fact, and we both know it, but maybe it is indeed time that people gave us the respect this parade is supposed to help provide for vets of that once "Dirty War." WWII was the "Good War", see. We were the guys who came home stained.

It seems that everyone is finally coming around. And who were we, Orphan and me, to disappoint the adoring throngs?

They say Westy will really be there. I never saw him when I was in-country. I never saw anybody much, except for the people I fought with, and against, and the people I partied with during R and R in Saigon. It was a select few.

James Hugh Marten was a Spec Four and I was his Staff Sergeant. That's the way we both came home. Orphan never got laced, and I only got a taste of shrapnel where I sit. The guy who set off the mine came home in pieces. I mean the guy who set off the mine from which I received a souvenir.

"You think I'm drunk, Indian?"

"Is this some kind of freaking quiz? Of course you're goosed, fool."

"Come on, Gary. If you like, I'll switch to Diet Coke and we will drive like hell into that city. Just in time to make our big moment."

"This ain't anything to be sarcastic about. This is something that needs a little dignity to—"

"How many years have gone by?"

"I know the argument. It don't mean nothin'."

"Don't give me the stock booshwah, Indian. Mr. Three Bears. I'll bet you took incredible shit over that surname, back in school."

"I did."

"I did...Did they ask you where freaking Goldilocks was?"

"All the time. Until I started sporting a switchblade in my sock. And then they all went back to asking me where an Indian got a name like Gary."

"You're a funny man, Sarge. A very funny man."

We're sitting at a picnic table. There is a brown shopping bag containing our twelve pack of Coors on top of the table, between us. He's done most of the imbibing. There are four empties in front of him, and he's put away a pint of scotch, as well. So I've been doing most of the driving through South Dakota, and South Dakota is where we still are, I make it.

We are alone, this morning. No one else is at the picnic tables. The only visitors to the rest stops have been people who are using the piss tubes. Everybody seems to be in a big hurry to get somewhere.

But not us, currently.

"You want to make this parade, or do you want to go somewhere else? It won't break my heart if we don't—"

"The hell it won't, Sarge. It'll break your heart. And we're gonna get there. Just let me finish this last beer, and we'll be on our way. When we get into Iowa, I'll be straight enough to take over the controls."

"It's seven, James. A.M. This thing begins at one. We got the

whole state of Iowa and the top one-third of northern Illinois to get across if we're going to make it."
"We will. It don't mean nothing" he says.
"Let's get away from the war for a minute."
"Can't get away from it. Isn't that why we're hitting Chi?"
"Let's get away from it anyway."

His face mellows. It isn't harsh-looking anymore. It's almost like a chemical Jekyll and Hyde change, I'm thinking.
"What gets your mind off Nam?" he asks.
"Women used to."
"What do you mean? Bar girls sneaking into your hootch on the perimeter at night or something?"
"No. I mean girls from home."
"You mean your first wife?"
"Nah, hell, nah. I don't mean that vicious bitch. I mean my first lady."
"You mean your first piece."
"That's a harsh and inaccurate way to put it."
"What other way is there to put it, Indian? Isn't that the way you put it to her?"
"And I thought you were mellowing out."
He casts his eyes toward the hand with the can in it.
"I don't know why I'm dumping on you this way," he says.
"Neither do I."
"You would've fragged my ass, back in Bong Son."
"No, Orphan, I wouldn't have fragged you."
He shoves the beer can aside. Some of the brew sloshes out off the top lip of the can.
"All right. Talk to me and sober me up. Then we'll be on our way. This moosepiss has done enough talking out of my mouth. Tell me about your first lady."
"You really want to hear?"
"I wasn't lying, Indian. Tell it."
"I ain't going into any gory details."
"I like a story with subtlety."
"Fine. Whatever that means."
"It means you don't have to describe the gush-gush."

"Not me, Orphan. I never kiss and spread around the gynecological details. No sir."

"Come on. Tell it anyway."

"Shirley."

"Shirley?"

"What's wrong with Shirley?"

"I thought a lusty Indian like you, a Cheyenne brave, would have had a Mexican lass. Someone like a Miranda or a Carmelita."

"You must be high, Jimmy. There were Bohunks and Germans in our town. We were the minority, the Mexes and us."

"White guys."

"Just as lily white as thee."

"You're digressing. Shirley."

"Shirley. Sixteen years old. We're parked in the old man's pickup. We'd been swimming at the strip mines near Peregrine Lake. You know it?"

"We fished there, didn't we?"

"Yeah. There it is. So we're done swimming, it's the fourth month I've been taking this blonde Bohunk out, and I'm figuring it's time I made my move."

"And you did."

"No graphic details. Remember?"

He raises his hands in surrender.

"I worked my way to the top of her red bathing suit. It was one of those one piece suits, but it wasn't one of those grungy numbers with the little skirts that only nerdy females wear, or females with fat asses. I've noticed that at the beach."

James purses his lips in disgust.

"All right, all right. So her top comes down and my eyes get wide as moons and nature takes its course."

"Was she a natural blonde?"

"You had to be there."

"Very funny."

"Who knows? It was the last time we went out. She was afraid some Indian was going to give her a Cheyenne papoose. Her lust only went as far as the pigment line."

"Then why'd she go out with you in the first place?"

"Who knows? I used to be a good-looking sucker. The girls

always thought I had Latin blood."

"Is that what Shirley thought?"

"She wanted to live dangerously. Once was enough, I guess." He looks disappointed.

"Well, what the hell did you think happened? Moonlight in freaking Tahiti? Springtime in the Sierras? April in Paris?"

"July at the strip mines."

"Shirley at the gate."

We both laugh loud and long.

"We're never going to make this frigging parade. We're going to miss Westy, Orphan."

"Was it painful?"

"For her? Nah, she was a big heifer."

"Jesus Christ. You can be goddam dense.'

"That kind of painful?"

"Yes."

"You mean the 'first time' kind of painful?"

"Yes."

"You got to ask questions more carefully, Jimmy. Sure. I guess. But it didn't leave any of them psychological scars, if that's what you mean. If you mean do I compare all my other women with my first one."

"But you have to, don't you? It's the easiest one to remember because it's the first."

"What's the matter, Counselor? Did you have a bad number, your first time out?"

"My wife was my first. And she would've been my only if it hadn't been—"

"For Saigon. I remember. Hey, it happens. Twelve months on another planet, what do you expect to happen?"

"She wasn't a virgin when we made love."

"So what, man. This is the eighties. You are an experienced man of the world, now. And you had your own little indiscretion in a cat house in Ho Chi Minh City. Screw it. It's old business. Like Shirley. I can't even remember what kind of aureoles she had."

"Aureoles?"

"You know. The little circles around—"

"I know what the hell they are. Jesus, Indian. Aureoles."

"All this one-time cherry talk has you all whacked up. What's the matter with you?"

"I think I'm ready to hit the road. The parade, remember?"

"Sure. Don't you want to squeak a leak first? It's a long drive."

"Yeah. In a minute. Aureoles. Jesus."

I take a Coors out of the sack. They're becoming lukewarm.

"The beer's getting pissy. I finish this one, we trek into Iowa."

"The way you trekked into Shirley?" he asks.

"What?"

"Plunge ahead. The way you did it."

He's smiling like the juice is doing the talking for him, again.

"You been doing any prime time sloshing at home by yourself, Jimmy?"

"I never drink alone. And I don't go out with anyone, either. Cee and I stay home with the baby. We like to."

"Good. Good."

He's got hold of his discarded beer, once more, but then he puts it aside for the second time.

"Cee knew what there is to know. She taught me everything. And then I had to get into it with those slobs in Saigon. You realize I could've been true to the only goddamn woman in my life if it hadn't been for them?"

"You ever tell the old lady that war story?"

"No," he answers.

"Good."

"I lost my cherry in her brother's apartment, at Notre Dame."

"Under the Golden Dome."

"Shit. You didn't lose your cherry at that strip mine and I didn't lose mine under that Golden Dome."

I look at him with a question on my face, but then that cloud passes, and my querying expression dissolves.

"Yeah, I guess not," I say.

"We lost them there. Didn't we? In country. Left a red stain on all that California-like greenery. But it wasn't California, was it?"

"Take it easy, Orphan."

He was raised by a priest until he left for college. Then he left for the war. He was all on his own, most of his life. The priest left the priesthood and married an ex-sister. The padre is now godfather to Jimmy's children. He lives out near James, near San Fran.

"Cherries come in bunches, and that's the way they're lost...I'm all right. And I'm through with this beer. Drink up. Shirley. Indeed. Shirley."

I finish the Coors, as commanded. He picks up the sack with the remaining cans, and we toss our empties into the wastecan. The sign about "Give A Hoot, Don't Pollute" is nailed to the tree by the garbage container.

"What the hell's so funny about a name like Shirley?" I demand.

But he climbs up into the passenger's side of his red Chevy van.

When I get in, I put the key into his ignition.

"Iowa. Coming up shortly," I tell him.

"Shirley. Jesus. Shirley."

And he laughs while I pull us out into the thickening interstate morning traffic.

THE GULF OF MEXICO

She has her fingers poking out the air vent. She's tapping on the glass with her fingers and she's keeping rhythm with the radio by thumping her left foot on the floorboard. The music is Dave Brubeck. A famous old jazz thing called *Take Five*.

I used to have all his old albums, at college. All those experimental jazz albums that he did in 5/4 time (and a few other weird times). I liked Joe Morello, on the drums, best. In fact, I saw him break both drumsticks while he was pounding out *Castilian Drums* at a college concert. The man was fantastic. When he brought you back to that simple 4/4 beat, in the middle and at the end of his solo, the entire joint went berserk. And most of the audience had to be rock and boogie fans. Jesus, he played hell out of those drums. Looked like a little businessman, too. Like somebody at your door peddling Mutual of Omaha or All State or State Farm.

That hamburger is rising back up on me. After all that heavy feed I put down at the reception, I had to have a Super-Dooper-Double-Meat-Lumberjack-Special. And now my bowels have to pay the price. She's the one who really wanted to stop. She's got this thing for roadside all-night greasy spoons. I could've waited to find a McDonald's or a Hardy's or a Prince Castle, but she likes her joints seedy. Says the goddam truckdrivers really do know where the good food's at.

Indiana is as flat as Illinois. That's why it's got so much good farmland. When you don't have to rip up boulders and rocks and mountains, it makes it a little easier for the farmers to grow things. If the pilgrims had landed in Indiana, Thanksgiving wouldn't have been such a great big deal. The harvest would've come a bit too easily. And the Indians probably would've been a little softer than the east coast breed of natives.

You've got to watch out for the Indiana State Troopers. They're tough. Tougher than the Illinois State Cops. Indiana cops won't give you five miles over the limit, so I keep my eyes on the speedometer.

I don't know how I can drive more than five miles at a time. Not when I think about how taut every muscle in my body is. You could bounce a quarter off either of my forearms. You'd think I'd be exhausted after a few minutes, but I've been driving for three and a half--no, four hours, now. With only that one stop. Hell, we're just about into Kentucky.

Three hours into Kentucky, and the sun's about to come up. It's almost 6:15. And Dee Dee's hungry. But I refuse to stop in one of those hog wallows, again. This time we're going to eat with table cloths and napkins and clean silverware. We're going to stop in a joint that has some kind of faintly recognizable name over its door.

When I drive and think about stuff other than the road and the lines and the stripes down the middle of the road, the miles and the time go quickly. If I think about the wedding and the reception, or even about some rotten archaic softball game I've played in, it seems like we're suddenly ready to stop and fill my Pontiac again.

It's been hot and sticky all day and all night, and I can feel the thermometer getting ready to start its upward hike today, even though it's only 6:25. It's going to be a real bastard. If we're lucky, we'll make it to Macon before dark.

It's time to stop and fill up anyway, so we might as well pull up at the *Happy Day Motor Haven.*. There's a fairly hygenic looking restaurant here, and a gas station and a car wash. So, I pull in and stop by the pump, and then hand the attendant my keys. He gives me a wash ticket when I tell him to fill it up. He gives me receipt number 1113.

There are a number of families in the restaurant, and there are some godawful looking locals (locals, I guess, anyhow) sitting at the snackbar. The locals look like farmers or construction workers. I can't tell which. Some of them are wearing Choo Choo Charley engineer hats, the hats with the puffed up tops and long bills and the light gray stripes. And most of them are wearing bib overalls. I see one of them sipping and slurping out of his coffee cup. His doughnut is submerged in the coffee, and he bites and slurps in one continuous gulping motion. He has nine o'clock shadow. Big mean looking sucker.

They're really not all miniatures of each other, but they do all smack of being from Hoopers, Kentucky. Christ. Hoopers, Kentucky.

They have six or seven rows of long rectangular tables (in sets of three, end to end) in the middle of the floor. All the booths are taken, of course, by the denizens of Hoopers, so we're going to be stuck sitting close to a family of four. It's 6:45, and the damned joint's packed. So, we sit.

The family of four sounds like a northern bunch, to our relief. At least we're not going to have to listen about life and times in northern Kentucky or about manure spreaders or...

"Robert, sit up and drink your orange juice. If you want to eat any pancakes, you're going to drink every ounce of that expensive juice. Go on, drink it.

"Maryann, you too. Will you please leave the silverware alone? Where did you get that pen? Stop writing on that doily!"

"Jeanine, will ya please let them destroy the joint? Just so we can have one quiet meal before we finally get home? Please?"

"Why are you so crabby? I drove three hundred and twenty-five miles last night, Nicholas, if you remember. These children are going to do as they're damned well told if I—"

"Christ, you had to drive instead of doing your goddam Scrambles, and now you're never gonna let me—"

"Robert, drink THAT JUICE and stop putting your little finger in your mouth!"

"Aw, let him put his finger all the way up his nose, if he wants."

"Don't start that gross business, mister, at seven o'clock in the morning."

"Look, we're all tired. Let's just ease off."

"Don't tell me to ease off. Just because you've absolutely

ruined our vacation . I don't care who hears all this. And when we get back to Ann Arbor, you can fill these children with soda pop and cheeseburgers, but right now they're going to drink their goddamned orange juice."

"Shut it down, Jeanine. Let these other poor people have some peace, willya? You can do all the screaming you want when we roll up the windows and put on the air conditioner and get fifty miles out of goddam HOOPERS, Kentucky, GODDAMMIT!"

"Daddy, please don't yell. You're not posta yell. Mommy —"

"You butt out, young lady, If Daddy and Mommy want to discuss, then you'll just have to —"

Dee looks like she's swallowed some coffee, from a cup with a surprise cigarette butt at the bottom.

"Hey, there's a booth open."

We move and take the booth across the dining room floor, and as I sit down, I see Nicholas and his Empress Jeanine still splattering spittle at each other, in a muffled volume, now. I guess they don't want the rest of the world to know that they were both born on top of a perpendicular pickle.

"What horrible people. Are we ever gonna be like them?"

"No," I insist. I won't argue with her like that. I sneer and tell her that I'll just lock her and her vermin children in the basement.

I order coffee and toast. That "Lumberjack" hamburger is still with me. Dee orders the Breakfast Special: pancakes and sausages and eggs (easy over, she says) and toast and milk and orange juice and coffee. She's going to get sick just because there's a special $1.49 deal going on here.

Our waitress is beyond the menstrual gloom of her late forties. She has some silver hair, some tremendously apparent breasts, and skinny, bird-like legs. She's friendly, though. I didn't expect that anywhere south of Gary, Indiana. And those breasts are simply gargantuan and out of place, on an otherwise frail body. I imagine she has one helluva Saturday night working here, when the bar's open. But I don't see any of the Choo Choo Charlies giving her anything more than a cordial nod as she refills their coffee mugs or as she slips their check in a dainty, almost girlish way, next to their silverware.

I love to watch people cook. I especially liked that whacko English guy who used to gallop all over afternoon T.V. I even enjoy watching the women slap the tiny hamburger patties on the grill at White Castle. It staggers me to see people handling food in such a mechanical, precise way. I know there's no loving touch in a hash house, at the hands of a short order grill man, but I like to watch them fix the food. Somehow it's attractive to me.

I used to order tuna fish sandwiches after numerous, horrendous drunks on Saturday nights at college. I'd become hellaciously hungry after trying to soak up a half barrel of beer. And my pals used to get equally as hungry, and we'd all invade the First Street greasy spoon, well after midnight.

I could think of nothing but tuna fish, amid all the cheeseburgers and fried eggs and french fries and onion rings and cheese omelets and ham 'n cheese sandwiches and grilled cheese sandwiches and Italian beef and Italian sausage sandwiches. I have to have tuna fish. I salivated over the stuff without benefit of a bell. And *mis amigos, los borachos,* always became angry at my order of "two tuna fish salad sandwiches on rye" (with a side order of kosher dills).

"How the hell can you put that catfood inside yourself, Freddy? You're a goddam alleycat."

The waitress there had big boobs, too, and big legs and big butt. She wasn't dainty and dusty and nostalgic and odd like this waitress in Hoopers, Kentucky. I think I'm in love with her. Dee, if you're reading my skull, tune out now, won't you?

I love all people who work in joints like this. The cooks and the waitress and the girl at the candy-checkout counter. They're the veins of this goddam country. They feed us more than food. They're somehow together, one and the same, in Illinois and Kentucky and Indiana.

I watch her eat. She goes after the sausages first, then the eggs, the toast, the pancakes. She vacuums her plate in a clockwise pattern. And she finally sops up the egg yolk with her toast. When she's finished, she looks up miserably, at me.

"Why did you let me order and eat all this?"

The girl at the cashier's counter is probably seventeen or eighteen years old. She rings up our bill on the cash register, first. Then, she re-adds the bill on a small electric adding machine, and she skewers the tallied slip on a slender inverted spike.

I hand her a five dollar bill and she turns to the cash register.

She places the bill on the metal edge, above the cash drawer. She counts out two singles and 78 cents in change. And she re-counts the cash in the palm of my hand, "Three, Four..... Seventy, Eighty, Ninety... Five dollars. Thank yew." She has a split between her two upper front teeth. A wide gap. And she's wearing black, horn rimmed bifocals. There's a mole on her right cheekbone, and there are hairs growing from the blemish.

There are also a half dozen huffing, annoyed paying customers angrily waiting behind us. I feel like turning on them and smashing in their stinking faces.

"Thank yew agin, sir. Come agin."

My Pontiac is sitting next to the wall of the car wash. It is hopelessly and bravely trying to shine after its bath. I can almost see the teeth of the grill forcing a grin at me. But the rust spots merely come off a bit more clay red than they were when we started this trip.

The gas bill of $8.55 is paid, and the small stringy blond teenager offers me a Mr. Magoo drinking glass or a box of Tide or a package of Puffs. I take the Puffs. When he hands me the tissues, I see his red-stoned high school ring, but I can't make out the words and the date. He has aqua eyes. Dee takes the tissue from me.

They have a dog in the service station. He looks like a German Shepherd, but the face is just a little bit wrong. Like some mutt mated with his nice pure Aryan bitch-mother. He's big and he has charcoal and silver fur. And he's slobbery. I feel like asking him, "Ver ah your papuhs?". The dog gives me an annoyed Nazi "Sieg!" with his left front paw, as he flops down on his side, next to the drinking fountain.

The kid with the stringy hair counts the change in my hand, too. I think he's peeking at my city sticker, on the windshield. I've never seen such careful, purposeful people. Southern hospitality, baby.

Kentucky seems like a skinny state, since we're cutting across it from north to south. It's fairly green, and once in a while it's hilly. (I'm getting very tired of flat farmland.) And when we drive through the middle and southern half of the state, the scenery begins to pick up.

We pass by a few thoroughbred farms. The horses seem dignified and proud looking. More dignified than the burros you see faking it at Arlington or at Belmont. They've got their heads thrust upward and erect and they trot pompously all over that fenced in grass. What a life. The life of a stud. Sounds like the title of a porno book.

Goddam horses.

I keep watching the temperature gauge. Every time the red bar tickles its way past the halfway mark, I start thinking about turning the heater on. To release the heat from under the hood. But when I fiddle with the blower button, Dee tells me, "It isn't going to overheat while we're moving, Freddy. Believe me."

"Oh yeah," I'm saying to myself. So, I leave the heater alone. But my eyes keep wandering back to the small red bar every three or four miles.

How many things can go wrong with a machine? The tires, the engine, the brakes, the transmission, the radiator, the exhaust system. Jesus, I have a picture of my car being towed into Florida with all its tires flattened and with my tail pipe banging on the pavement. And all she can say is, "Believe me."

Kentucky. Kentucky......Tennessee. "Tennessee welcomes you." Tennessee is another skinny north to south crossover. Five, six hours to cross, is all.

It's almost noon. I look at her and I know what she's thinking. So I tell her I'm hungry, to break the pattern. She smiles at me, with her curly kinky hair flowing and blowing across her eyes, and some of the strands become trapped in her mouth. She grasps the ends of her hair and makes spitting sounds as she clears the curls from her lips. She rolls up her window.

Standall's Standard Oil (And Restaurant).

We're about thirty-five miles into Tennessee. Maybe we can still make it to Macon by dark. Depends on the traffic in Georgia. Up till now the road's been clear and fast. And the weather's been clean, too.

There are plenty of open booths in this little cafe. But no Choo Choo Charlies. I'm almost disappointed. Our waitress is young and brunette and small breasted and unattractive. She isn't wearing glasses and her teeth are pearl and as straight as a picket fence. What a letdown.

Hunger has returned to me. As it always does. I'm thinking about ordering — you know what I'm thinking about ordering. But I'm not sure these guys make it with celery and onion and boiled eggs and real mayonnaise. So I chicken-out and order two cheeseburgers and large fries and a large Coke.

The heat's made me thirsty. A beer would really be it, right now, but all that driving remains. See, I can't drink one beer, or eat one hamburger or gobble one potato chip. I've got the impulse to do everything big. Eating, drinking, working, playing. Sex. All those things I have to do BIG. Even if I'm not very hungry or very thirsty or very horny or very ambitious. "The Plague," I call it. No matter what you own or absorb, it's gotta be lots. You gotta win all the gold medals, screw all the cheerleaders, and drink all the beer in the barrel.

I guess it has something to do with Yankees being goal happy. Hell, success and winning and the Super Bowl. The idea is to never let anybody else win. Look at Vince Lombardi and the New York Yankees of the 30's and 50's; and that mustache-Pete, that Mark Spitz. They all hogged the glory, and that makes them great. They're the real American Winners.

Look, if you hit three for four on Sunday and go zero for four on Monday, on Monday night they're all saying, "What's he done for us lately?"

Anyway, that's why I order two cheeseburgers and the large fries and the large Coke.

I pick up a copy of a Memphis newspaper at the cashier's counter. I almost buy it, but I figure, "What kind of sports page are they gonna have?" Maybe news about the ponies or about Buford Pusser and his magic ball bat, but that's about it. I put it back on the rack.

Dee ate very little. Just a chicken salad sandwich and a glass of milk. She changed her order twice, too.

She's obsessed with her weight. Every time she gains three pounds, she has to go on a diet and lose fifteen pounds. That's her mathematics.

I'm sure I know why she's nervous about the calories this time, though.

There was a fat woman sitting all by herself at one of the four rectangular tables in the center of the dining area. She was wearing a dress that looked exactly like a khaki army pup tent. The dress extended down to the middle of her calves. The only exposed flesh of hers that was visible was her fatty globby neck and her bulbous fingers and her fleshy forearms and her watermelon sized upper arms. She was eating cottage cheese and saltine crackers, and she was drinking a glass of iced tea.

She was eating doggedly slow. Just the way they told her to at the doctor's or at Weight Watchers or at some damned place. And I'll bet they told her, "There's a skinny woman living inside that fat woman's body of yours." And I'll bet she gets down on her knees at night and asks God to keep chocolate and candy and bread and potatoes out of her mouth and stomach. I'll bet she asks God to help keep her chubby fingers off the refrigerator handle and she asks Him to let the flesh melt off her bones and I'll bet she asks Him to stop all those kindly stares from her friends and relatives when she puffs and gasps up any flight of stairs. She asks God why she can't be a normal person and why she can't be attractive and why she has to lust after marshmallows and peanut butter and why, God, why she can't be like everybody else.

She eats her cottage cheese with a teaspoon, slowly and carefully. She cuts her slice of lettuce with the edge of her spoon and eats it in her plodding, stalling way. She sips her iced tea in short sporadic swallows and she tugs on her khaki tent, near the thighs, trying to lower it to her ankles.

When Dee gets a full load of the fat woman sitting at that table in the middle of the floor, she rapidly changes her order, in sequence, from steakburger-to Reuben-to chicken salad. When her food comes, she eats slowly too, and she tugs at her bluejeaned thighs. She doesn't look at me until she's finished.

Food. Jesus, I'm sick of it. I want to swim in the pool at the Holiday Inn in Macon. I want to run in the white sand on the Gulf in Sarasota, and then on the beach of one of the Keys. I want to feel sweat running from me, and feel my stomach being sucked in by exhaustion.

Like it used to be in Michigan. I'd be in the lake for two hours straight. My old man would have to come in and drag me out before my skin shrivelled up and turned purple.

And at night I'd read 25 cent Superman and Batman and

Captain America comic books. There'd be no T.V. in our cottage, up in Michigan. The nights were almost cold, and I always slept soundly through the night. The nights were tar black. I couldn't see my fingers in front of my face.

The beach was everything for six or seven days. I wanted to get out on the sand at 7:00, but they made me wait till 10:00, so that the sun would warm everything up.

Vacations aren't the same anymore. You count your change now, and you fill up the gas tank, and you have to figure how much you have left to spend.

I'm driving at 60, right on the button. If we were able to go back to the 70 limit, this trip'd take about four hours less. I figure the total driving time to Sarasota is around 25 or 26 hours. Once we get past Georgia, we've got it made.

Once we get past Georgia. Yeah, once we pull over and crawl into a gas station and get my right rear fixed. I didn't notice anything until the steering wheel started to pull, about ten minutes ago. It must be a small leak that turned into a yawning hole.

At least it's no blowout.

I drive about 30, in the right hand lane. The sign says, "Gas—One Mile." I hope to Jesus that we're not riding on the rim. That would end our little holiday real quick.

We pull in slowly and stop near the windowed sliding doors of *Jim and Marion's Texaco*. There are two cars being serviced at the moment. They're both up on the hydraulic lifts.

With a bit of good fortune, though, the Mercedes on the right is about to be lowered. They've finished changing the oil and the oil filter. The mechanic operating the lift has his back to us. He's working the lever that lets the damned thing down.

He's very short and very skinny, and he has straight and long black hair. I didn't expect to see much long hair in Tennessee. Until he turns around and he has a cloth, sewn-on name tag that reads '*Marian*'.

"Tire, right?"

She's greasy and dirty and sweaty. And pretty. Almost beautiful. Dee takes one look and decides to head for the john. The look she gives Marian is perfectly feline. Like a female alley cat coming eye to eye with another female alley cat. It almost makes me tense.

"Yeah. The right rear."

I'm absolutely brilliant when I come upon this kind of woman. I feel awkward and stupid. She ain't a lady wrestler.

She has blue eyes. I see them when she hoists my Pontiac up on the lift and as she's examining the tread for a puncture mark. Her lips are thin and faintly pink. She's slight and almost gaunt, and there's hollowness in her cheeks. I can imagine that her hair's straight and raven black when she washes it. She lowers the car until the tires are all touching the ground. Then she starts unscrewing the lugnuts with one of those power 'unscrewers,' or whatever.

She's quick. She takes the tire over to a work bench to patch it up, and then she looks up at me with a mouth full of white Hollywood teeth.

"You're from Illinois, huh?"

"Yeah. Yeah, Chicago."

"Jim and I are from Minnesota. Outside of St. Paul. Came and started up here in Galva in — it must have been three and a half years ago. Where are you heading?"

"Florida. And the Keys. We're gonna stay in Sarasota for a couple of days."

"Hotter 'n a bitch right now. Even a bit hotter than it is right here. The humidity's really bad. Watch out for the sun. It'll burn hell out a fair skinned guy like you."

"We just got married, yesterday. We've been driving ever since we got out of the reception. Drove all night. We thought we'd make it to Macon by tonight."

"You're just married, huh? I figure I might succumb to that madness some day. See, I write. I only screw around with this goddam gas station. There she is. Now all we gotta do is filler up and screw it back on the axle."

"Why do you work here? Like you were just saying?"

"Because my father, Jim there, that old goofy looking guy, needs somebody to help him out. And I work cheap. All I need's a roof and food and paper and pencil. And a few bucks to throw around, once in a while."

"What kinda stuff do you write?"

"Short stories and poems. And I started a novel."

"Had anything printed up?"

"Yeah. A story and a couple of poems. Some literary quarterly in southwest Texas."

"Well, hell, good luck."

"Thank you. Really. That's nice of you to say."

Her eyes are blue and her lips are rose pink. She's small and almost frail. Her fingers are spindly and skinny and her fingernails are nearly sawed off and buffed down to the flesh of her finger tips. She's wearing a white T-shirt underneath her dirty gray coveralls. And she's got a silver cross hanging out on her chest. It flopped out from her T-shirt when she bent over to put the tire back on. There is a small kidney shaped birthmark on the base of her neck. I have a rotten smothering compulsion to kiss it, to touch it.

Dee's back. I know that when I feel her right arm slip around and onto my left arm.

"How's it going?"

I pay Marian the $2.50. I ask her her last name—so I'll recognize her name when her novel or short story goes big-time. I tell her, in a miserable, obvious way, that I'll be able to tell my kids that I met somebody famous once. She smiles at my crippled speech and she thanks me again. Her eyes are dancing and laughing, laughing at me. I mutter "goodbye", and Dee and I get in the car. We pull out past the gas pumps and stop before we reach the street. I look in the rear view mirror, but I can't see her. She's gone. And the street's clear and we're pulling out.

It isn't long before we're in Georgia. Just about immediately we come upon hills that are caked with that famous red clay. The landscape is more attractive than I thought it would be, until we get about three miles north of a road construction site. Then we're going ten miles an hour, and we're bumper to bumper. We're hitting all the vacation traffic right now. This is the bottleneck that leads to Atlanta, and then on to northern Florida.

I can only hack the radio for forty minutes, once we get caught in the jam. It's 4:30 and I'm hallucinating about the swimming pool at the Holiday Inn again. Goddam. Can we ever make it past the greasy food and the flat tires and—the temperature gauge indicator is rising. I can hear those doom-laden words once more! "It won't overheat while we're moving. Believe me." I'm angry at her now. The red marker's up to the 3/4 mark. And it's beginning to edge its way toward the 7/8 mark.

"I've got to turn the heater on. I don't care about the 93 degrees and the 68% humidity. We're going to blow up pretty soon if I don't turn on the heater."

"Turn it on. Go on. The damned traffic can't stay like this all the way to Florida. I hope."

My feet are burning and sweat is torching a path from my neck to my groin. The seat underneath me is becoming soaked with my own juice. I turn the radio off in a snapping violent twist.

"Take it easy. It'll end soon."

"Believe me. Believe me." I hate those goddam words. Like she's trying to pacify me. Like I'm a twelve year old pimple-pocked kid.

"Open that goddam back window, willya, before we choke on our own goddam heat!"

She grins at me like she understands how stupid and tiresome I'm becoming. Like she's a fifth grade teacher who's being real paternalistic. And she says, "It's gonna be all right, all right" if I'll be just a little bit patient. Nothing's wrong. Nothing to be scared about. Let me take your hand for a while, she's saying, and then everything will be all right and everything will pass. ˉCalm down now, little Freddy.

"What in hell is the problem here? All these goddam people enjoy standing in line, the sonsabitches. Here, I'll add another note to your goddam harmony! Get your asses moving you MISERABLE BASTARDS!"

The red bar is brushing the top line. I've got the heater on full throttle. On hot.

"Quit honking that stupid horn. It's not going to make us move one bit faster, for Christ's sake."

I'm gonna grow up all right. I'm gonna take my tire iron and smash in a couple of windshields. I don't give a damn whose windshield I break, either. I can just sense the pleasure of feeling all that sparkly glass being crushed under one blow from the metal bar, as I whack and belt out a few Chevy, Ford, and Buick windshields.

God. I can't believe it. I can finally see the construction site.

Jesus, it's only about three blocks long. They've got single lane traffic for those three measly blocks.

Some of the work crew are sitting on the black and yellow striped 'horses,' as we pass the site. The workers appear to be amused by the tidal wash of cars. They ought to be. It's 5:30. Quitting time.

As soon as we're past the single lane traffic, I've got us back up to 60 m.p.h. When the heat indicator crawls back to midway, I turn the heater off. Dee won't look at me.

That large sign, that dark green and familiar fluorescent sign, is like an oasis in hell. I'm telling you, this is what I've been waiting for since we left the city.

I don't especially enjoy travelling. I become too tense, too nervous. The sights along the road go right on by me, because I've got my eyes on the pavement or on some gauge. And Dee is not about to forgive me very quickly for making an ass of myself. Not very quickly or very easily.

We lug our suitcases into room 459 like a pair of weary continental adventurers. I'm thinking that I'm not all that tired. It's only been a twenty-some hour journey, and it's not quite over yet. But I'm weary and worn and almost dehydrated. When I see the pitcher of ice water on the night stand, I rise like a bedraggled Humphrey Bogart at the end of *Sahara* and guzzle three glasses of water before Dee can moisten her lips. Then I apologize for everything else I've done today, too. She whispers a barely audible "O.K." I kiss her and squeeze her with both my arms. For the first time in some twenty-odd hours, we're both smiling.

The restaurant is worthy of all the garbage they feed you on their T.V. commericals. Even though it's 10:30, the food is all quite warm when it is served. The service is brisk and decent. We have a waiter, this time. Class, ain't it?

I order red wine with the dinner, and when the waiter returns, he brings us the ice-packed dark green bottle, and then he tells us that the Cold Duck is compliments of the management. Dee is really impressed. She's not hostile any longer. She looks free, like the wine. The trip seems just barely worth it now, and I'm aware that it's all because of this $3.50 bottle of cheap wine. But, it's our free, cheap wine.

It's 11:45. I turn the color set on and find nothing but Sherlock Holmes and John Payne and Merv Griffin and some guest host even I don't recognize. I turn the set off.

Would you believe that she's been in the john for twenty minutes? Doing what, I'm not certain. But I feel like shouting "Take One!" at her. Jesus, come out of there before you ruin the whole damned thing. Please don't come out of there in a goddam negligee, pink or black or beige. God, let her come out naked or in hair curlers or with white chalky crap all over her face.

She's naked. She turns off one of the two lit lamps by the bed. And she turns the still lit three-way bulb down to dim. Then she leaps on top of me and begins tearing my T-shirt off. I help her along, before she rips the damned thing. She's kissing me impatiently and I'm staring at her intent, tightly closed eyelids. She opens her eyes in the middle of the kiss. We're breathing together in a stage whisper and pressing our slightly opened mouths together.

She begins to laugh hysterically. Laughing out loud like a berserk lady straight out of the crackers farm. And so that we totally destroy what has been, up until now, an entirely French, Christ, Parisian night, I start laughing like a loon, too.

You can tell that you're in Florida as soon as you start seeing palm trees, and as soon as you begin seeing cattle grazing on sandy bottomed grass. The roadside orange stands are legion. And grapefruit is almost equally prominent.

We stop at one of the stands and drink two sixteen-ounce glasses of freshly squeezed orange juice, all for a whopping total of 20 cents. The pulp sticks to my lips and I have a time wiping the orange strands away.

They are selling stuffed alligators. Little ones, about two feet long. Dee doesn't like any kind of reptile, and neither do I. I can just see a few of these critters' relatives floating in the New York sewage system. I tell her that we're going to buy our parents some oranges and grapefruits, on the way back. And I tell her if I can find a live gator, I'm going to mail him to her goddam brother, Randy. The punk. She winces and waves me off, disgustedly.

We arrive in Sarasota around 2:00 P.M. My aunt lays lipstick all over the both of us and my uncle is urging us to hurry and eat and get to the beach while there's still good sun left.

My aunt's dinner is the usual sumptuous, as it always is in my Polish, high-caloric-content family. My uncle continues pressing us to hurry up and finish and get out to the Gulf, like there's no time left in the world.

The Gulf of Mexico really does have white sand on its beaches. The water is clean and clear and green-blue. The salt makes the water taste very bitter. (Like a damned fool, I taste it.) I wash my face at the edge of the water.

When I walk into the Gulf (Dee wants to work up a sweat first) I can feel the buoyancy, the lightness that the water seems to contain. I can see my feet and each of my crooked white toes in the shallow water. The water is comfortable and almost warm. I wash a thousand miles from my arms and legs and head and chest and waist.

I'm on my back, floating, and I feel the sun burning into me, making my forearms and the back of my hands feel prematurely prickly and hot. I'll burn up, like Marian said. I'll burn to a cinder and float away from the beach and drift out into the Gulf, and from there it will be south, south, south.

I'm floating on my back thinking about hot dogs and beach blankets and teenaged females and 76th Street Beach and the skyline of "duh Loop."

I stand up erect in the shallow water, and as I wade in toward the shore, I can see three women standing on the sand. They're each wearing one piece black bathing suits. One of them is fifty years old and has breasts which totally inflate the front of her suit. She has some silver, iron colored hair and she is smiling at me in a benevolent gaze—so kindly that I stop noticing her great chest. And I feel like I'm supposed to embrace her and ask her to sit down. I ask her to come sit down with me. I'm still standing in the shallow water. I walk toward her, as if to touch her shoulder, and she crumbles flat to the ground, like a levelled sand castle.

There are only two women standing on the beach.

The girl with the mole and the bifocals is asking me, at the edge of the water, to take her into the Gulf and to make love to her. She is shedding her swimsuit. But, when she is standing naked before me, I see that her body appears to be waxen or plastic. She is a boyish mannequin. She has no breasts, no genitalia. Everything from her neck to her feet is shiny and flat and plastic. When I look up at her eyes, she pleads with me, "Take me into the water."

As I wade toward her and reach out to her, at the edge of the water, I touch her hand. It is hard and stiff, and my hand literally jumps back to my chest. I look at my palm and study it. When I glance up again, she's gone.

Only Marian remains. And a flock of seagulls searching for crumbs on the sand. She has her back to me. I call out her name, but she does not turn to me. I stand planted in the shallow water ten feet from her. She doesn't turn around. The gulls are swooping and screaming past my ears. I'm a wooden stake driven down into the white sand. The salt water and the sun are eating me alive. Devouring me. Digesting me. Marian..... I can see her deeply tan kidney shaped birthmark. I want to touch it. She turns abruptly, and she's holding an unbound loose leaf manuscript. She's wearing wire rimmed glasses and she's going to speak.

"I want to read something to you."

A gulp of salt water rushes into my snoring, eliptical mouth and into my nostrils. I feel the abrasive scratching of pebbles and rocks against my back. I've been washed ashore.

Dee is standing over me. I can't see her face because the sun is perched directly over her right shoulder.

"I've come to rescue you. You're either gonna drown or you're gonna fry to a black chip in this Gulf."

"Yeah. I almost fell asleep out there. I damn near floated away. I felt light. I just about damn near floated off."

My wife is beautiful. She has curly, kinky brown hair and a rounded woman-body. Her smile shows one crooked tooth. Her lips are heavy and full and her arms and legs are muscular and strong. Her waist is small and her stomach is flat.

I ask her to come in the water. I ask her to come into the Gulf with me. I tell her to come in and bathe with me. I want her to swim and float with me.

I whisper a strange inaudible sentence to the surface of the water. She doesn't hear my sentence.

Thomas Laird

GREMLIN

I didn't know his name until I heard my father talking about him at the dinner table.

His name was Henry.

Why I come to think about him now is something I can't exactly explain. Now that I'm about to have my first baby. I'm due on Wednesday. This is Sunday.

And while I'm sitting on the lawn chair in our backyard watching our sheltie chase flying leaves, I think of Henry, and I think of me when I was in fifth grade.

He delivered our morning papers. I only occasionally saw him because he delivered the weekday papers at five-thirty, when he was on time. And if the paper didn't arrive by seven, my father would call his home and talk to a man who was only identified as Henry's brother. I thought my father was complaining to Henry's father, for a long time, and the idea of Henry being embarrassed by that call made me equally embarrassed.

Henry was the poor soul of our neighborhood. He was in the seventh grade, but I didn't find out until much later, again, that he was already eighteen years old.

They threw him out of our elementary school when he reached his eighteenth birthday. The story I heard was that he would have to finish his education elsewhere, that the schoolboard thought it "inappropriate" that a boy, a man, his age should still occupy a desk with a bunch of youngsters.

So they got rid of Henry around Valentine's Day, his birthday. He became a legal adult on the day of hearts.

When they dismissed him, he couldn't seem to get it clear in his mind. He would deliver his newspapers at 5:30 A.M. just so he would be able to make it to school on time. I don't know why Henry worried about punctuality when he stayed in third, fourth, fifth, and sixth grades, all for more than the usual one year per grade. Of course he became the joke of our school, and it was even difficult for the most professionally-visaged of our teachers to keep a straight face when the subject of Henry came up. And Henry came up as the butt of many jokes, when I attended that grade school.

Henry was punctual if nothing else. We had heard that he was really EMH, educable, mentally handicapped. But we didn't know what those letters and words signified, then. We knew he was different, and as children so often are, we were cruel and insensitive toward him.

However, we didn't have much opportunity to hand him any abuse because as soon as school let out, Henry was on his way to his afternoon route.

When I misbehaved, my father sent me to my room. That was about as heavy as his punishments ever became. My father's mother, my grandmother, lived with us, once my mother died. I was four when she died of an aneurism. She came to help out with me when Momma left, and she stayed on, thereafter. Still, my father was always the disciplinarian, never Grandma.

One time I do remember him losing his temper, though. He grabbed hold of me by my shoulders, and I felt the extent of his considerable man-strength. I never realized how powerful he was until he took hold of me and shook me. I was so frightened that I cried before he had time to mete out any real punishment to me.

I think he frightened himself by laying hands on me because he forgot why he was castigating me, and he told me to go watch television, something he never told me to do.

I bring up my father's outburst to explain why I remember Henry. Be forewarned that I have not lost my train of thought.

I was talking about Henry's absence from our school. He was always ahead of me in grade, so I never shared a classroom with him.

By the time I graduated, he was long gone. Disappeared. Someone else took over his paper route.

But when he was cut adrift from our midst, when he had turned eighteen, he refused to accept his dismissal, and he began hanging around the school ground. We could see him through the windows of our classroom, cavorting about the playground, hanging on the monkey bars, swinging on the swings.

When those activities began to bore him, he would approach our windows and peer in, with his mouth against the glass, making faces and puckering up, his mouth against the pane.

He would always begin his antics when he saw our teacher's back to him. And when she finally caught sight of his presence, she would walk across the hall to the principal's office and report him. By the time Mr. Granzslik got outside, Henry had vanished.

He was like a ghost. Perhaps that is why I remember him during these last days before I deliver. He was a remnant of my childhood. Something vague. Something half-remembered.

He was certainly not an integral part of my past or of my upbringing. I hardly knew him, as I say.

But there was one other episode that stands out in my memory of him.

After several teachers had made sightings of this desperado, Henry, kissing their classroom windows and generally raising havoc among a throng of pre-pubescents, our Mr. Granzslik decided it was time to deal summarily with Henry. So the next time he received a complaint about our resident gremlin, he called Henry's "brother" on the phone and warned him that the school was going to have the police arrest Henry for trespassing the very next time he disturbed any of our classes. I, of course, heard about our principal's threat long after the fact.

It seems Mr. Granzslik's warning had been truly taken to heart because two days later Henry made a raid on our school grounds once again.

He worked his way down a row of classrooms. We had such large windows in our rooms that we could see almost to the end of the building, in my classroom. And we were all aware of Henry as soon as he set foot on the cinders of the playground.

He skipped the usual frolic at the monkey bars and the

swingset to begin his trek from classroom to classroom, leaving a trail of pucker-marks down the line of windows.

A moment.

Why did I call him a ghost, or, perhaps, a gremlin? His appearance fit the bill, somehow. He was a short, squat, simian boy—or young man, I should say. He had brown hair and the same color eyes. Rather cowish eyes, I remember. And his hair was rumored to have been cut by his "brother" or "father" or whoever it was that he really lived with. It was a sort of flat-top haircut. It grew out fairly long in the winter, and it was chopped down to the white stubs in spring and summer.

So, indeed, he did appear to be the small demon from the forest. The troll, the gremlin, the twisted elf, perhaps.

For all that, he was not an ugly boy, nor did he have any of the usual characteristics of what was then called "mongoloid." He was simply and unusually small for his age. And yet he seemed very different from all the true children around him. He was neither Quasimodo nor Oliver Twist. It is sometimes very difficult to get him precisely fixed in my mind.

When he made it to our room, our teacher and, I'm sure, all the other neighboring teachers down the line of the slobbered-up windows were in the principal's office.

Henry spent a good deal of time entertaining our room. He hopped about on one foot as if he had a hot-toe, and then he pirouetted numerous times until we were all as dizzy as he was, with laughter. He ran from pane to pane, kissing the glass, and then he jumped backward and began his series of pirouettes once again.

We hoped Miss Crown would never come back to us, we were laughing so hard. And we were the fifth grade class, which goes to show what an effective performer Henry was.

We were all waiting for the boom to fall, of course. We had seen the wrath of Mr. Granzslic before. When he promised a punishment, it arrived on schedule. So we knew the police were on their way to jail our private campus clown.

The gremlin. The ghost.

Several of us went up to the windows to warn him to make his escape, to leave before the principal's SWAT squad arrived, or the county sheriff's police. But he paid us no mind and he continued to careen from window to window. The laughter had ceased when our Miss Crown re-entered our room, but the outdoor performance continued. He did his dance and his fine, twisting ballet for our young, second-year teacher, now. She walked over to the glass somewhat hesitantly and demanded that he leave.

Then he did something else that sticks to memory. He gave our young, inexperienced, about-to-be-wed teacher the finger.

I knew it was the finger because I had learned about that specific digit in the third grade from a bunch of low-talking third grade girls. They had picked it up from some fourth grade boys.

I saw Miss Crown blush, and then I saw a trapped look on her face. There was no one outside to make Henry stop. The principal was probably in his office waiting for the sheriff's officers. And she could not leave the room again because she had already made her complaint and report to the office. She also had to keep an eye on us, as we were her primary responsibility.

Yet she could not resume teaching us math. That was what we had begun before Henry's performance and outburst of the finger. And she could not take us outside because that was where this mini-monster still lurked.

We still could not see a police car out in our parking lot. Obviously, the sheriff did not consider Henry a threat to our safety. But he would have had he seen the face of Miss Crown. We all began to feel sorry for her, I am sure. We had all been rather non-commital in our feelings toward her since she was only a second-year teacher and had not yet made "her bones" into the mainstream of our school. Nevertheless, the woman was suffering, and we began to suffer along with her.

Then, a gray, beat-up station wagon appeared in our parking lot.

A man emerged from the wagon. He was indistinct to us at first, but gradually we were able to see the resemblance.

He had a potbelly and was wearing only a white t-shirt and gray work pants. It was cold and February and he wore no jacket, I recall.

Henry swung his head toward the lot when he heard the station wagon's door slam. The man approaching Henry did not say a word.

We could see that his lips remained shut.

Henry froze. His silly antics ceased immediately. We could not see his face, then, but I saw his arms simply go limp. They literally flopped to his sides.

He made no attempt to escape. The potbellied man came closer and closer until he stood before Henry, face to face, within arm's reach of him.

Then he swung ferociously at the squat, younger man. The blow made Henry reel backward. Someone screamed in our classroom, but it wasn't me. I could not breathe, just then, let alone allow a sound to burst from my mouth.

He swung at Henry again, and this time the paperboy fell to the ground.

Miss Crown tried to divert our attention from the windows. She promised that the police and our principal would end this nightmare outside our classroom.

No one ended it, just then. The fat man waited until the eighteen year old rose again, and then he slapped him once, twice, and then a third time, backhanded.

Henry shrieked. It is the only sound I can distinctly remember hearing out of him for as long as I knew him. I didn't know how to categorize the sound of his voice. It wasn't quite human, but it certainly wasn't lupine, either. It was a scream of—of indignity, I think. It wasn't as if he were in any particular pain. It was as if this interloper, this fat, t-shirted man, had interrupted something that was privately Henry's and Henry's alone.

He slapped Henry three more times, and the boy's protesting bellow ceased. It was as if someone had suddenly dropped a grand piano into the middle of our classroom. There was a silence that was one point beyond 'awful'. We could not breathe At least I could not.

Miss Crown almost fainted. Three boys finally came to her aid. They sat her down at her desk, and one of them went out after water.

While we were watching Miss Crown regain her senses, our eyes were taken from the two men outside. When we returned our attention to the windows, they were gone.

Henry was still our paperboy for some months after his 'altercation' on our schoolgrounds, but I never saw him again. Five-thirty was too early for me, then. I never saw the sun rise until I went to an overnight party in the sixth grade.

We knew he had gone when we received a card from the newspaper with the name of our new carrier.

He never returned to the schoolgrounds for a repeat performance, and Miss Crown never mentioned that trying day to us again.

Our Miss Crown married and she became, by the time I graduated, one of the most popular instructors at our elementary school. Mr. Granzslik went on to become the superintendent of our district.

I went on to graduate from an expensive college, and I have a career in commerical art that hasn't been interrupted by my pregnancy. My husband is a tax lawyer. He also writes mystery stories, none of which have been published. But he is undaunted, and he keeps sending them out.

I find it strange that I should remember Henry just now. My due date is soon. Although my doctor has miscalculated by the usual two weeks, I'm sure this is the week our baby will come.

Remembering my father's firm grip on my shoulders and recalling the near-savage beating that our resident gremlin took in front of the student body somehow do not seem to coincide, to touch. And yet I feel them intersect now, as I sit on an orange, mesh lawn chair in our backyard.

If he hadn't frightened me so badly, I might even think that I miss Henry. And perhaps his potbellied "brother" as well. Certainly I miss Miss Crown and even the widely-feared Mr. Granzslik.

We, of course, have a paperboy in our new neighborhood. His name is Andrew, and he is quite a handsome little boy.

He is an honor student and a wonderful little league baseball player, I am told. He's been pushed ahead a grade, and he's an all 'A' student.

I saw his father pick him up after he delivered our block's newspapers one Saturday morning. His father was obviously the genetic pool from which Andrew sprung. Tall, stately. A professional man of some sort. I've never seen Andrew's mother. But I can imagine her.

There are mornings, however, that I have anticipatory fear that I'll open our front room curtains and I'll find lip marks on our picture window.

When I opened those curtains this morning, I looked the glass over carefully. Then the baby kicked inside me, and out of the corner of my eye I thought I saw a short, brown figure dart toward our neighbor's bushes. But Andrew had already delivered our morning edition, and I laughed out loud.

I peered far down the street, and indeed there was nothing to see.

But I quickly closed the curtains and I sat down and cried foolishly, and even my husband's most soothing consolation could not quiet me and my grief.

THE EDGE

They weren't listening to him. He found that they never listened to him. They knew he was a substitute and not the real thing, and he knew that they knew that he didn't have any leverage over them.

He had been assigned to take boys' shop. He was a history teacher, grades 9 through 12, but he had been assigned woodshop for freshman high school boys.

They were of mixed races, some white, some black, some Hispanic. None of them were Jewish. But he was. Mort Klein. His friends in college always asked him what changes his father's name had gone through when his father came to this country, but he was a fourth generation American Jew.

They were talking loudly as he entered the sawdust-laden classroom, but when they saw the small, banjo-string-thin man walk into their room, the noise became a maelstrom. This was how it normally went, Mort figured.

He thought, "Now I have to threaten them with the dean. And if that doesn't work, maybe I'll have to actually bring the dean into the room with them. But deans never like that. It makes me look—" But he was interrupted by a wooden ruler that became a dangerous missile that nearly knocked his wire rimmed glasses from his face.

"Now look! I won't tolerate this noise. If you want me to get the dean to come in here and babysit, I will."

Another ICBM, made of wood and having both the metric system and the foot and inches designations flew over the top of his head. They were very professional about it, he thought. When he put his eyes on the left hand side of the metal shop tables, the ruler would of course come out of the right side's periphery. He could never quite locate the culprit. He had been through this before.

They quieted down slightly with the threat of the entrance of the dean of boys. Now Mort knew he had found a slight edge. But he knew also that he couldn't overplay the bit about fetching the administration. He knew they would figure he would be sent home if he couldn't control them by himself. And that would be forty dollars pay down the tubes. Without the substitution money coming in, Mort wouldn't be able to pay his share of the rent with his girlfriend, Mira. It was a flexible relationship, but she was a great materialist, he knew, and just because they slept together once in a while didn't mean that she would allow him to let her pay the bills.

If Mort worked five days a week, he made about $160, take home. In fact he was doing very well at that wage. He had been able to take Mira out to dinner several times lately. After he had been working regularly for a month, it was the middle of November, he had found Mira's ad in the *Sun-Times* for a roommate. It didn't list the fact that Mira was a female, but it didn't take Mort long to gear himself to the idea of a female roomie, once he saw that she was his type of female. She didn't have imposing breasts. He could not stand large breasts. She had a perfect waistline, no flab at all. He could not adapt to fat since he was an ex-failure at gymnastics in high school, himself. And best of all she looked Jewish. Since Mort felt that he looked Jewish, he figured Mira would be a sure thing.

But there was nothing sure about her, he found out. He had only just made love to her two months ago (it was now March) for the first time. She had had more than a few men stay overnight in her bedroom (they each had their own bedroom, and there was an extra bedroom that they used as a T.V. room-study).

He had occasionally felt embarrassed when he walked out the door toward a substitution, nearly colliding with a number of aryan-looking males. It seemed that they were on their way to work, as well. Mort could not understand how she could hold a job and fornicate so freely on weeknights. If he didn't get ten hours of sleep, he couldn't face waiting for a telephone to ring at 6:30 in the morning.

The phone would ring and the board of education operator would tell Mort which horrifying section of the city he would be off to, to try and quell adolescent fury in a classroom. Because substituting was the bottom of the ocean, whale shit, where the leviathans rest in peace. Mort was convinced it was true.

But he was on his way to a fulltime position somewhere, and this gypsy existence of hopping from one acneed storm to the next wasn't going to last forever. Maybe just this one last year, Mort figured.

He was careful about turning his back. He turned his back to them only while he wrote the few chalked-upon-the-board words. He had been told only two things about his job by the man downtown who had certified him as a sub.

"Don't turn your back on them. And never smile."

So he never did. Turn his back or smile, that is.

There was a change of classes every hour. The first hour classes never seemed to be much trouble. They were usually too sleepy to cause any extended disturbance. But the worst trouble seemed to come after lunch. Then they seemed to become more restless and more prone to outright violence.

Mort had spent two days in the hospital, at the end of January. Some Hispanic kid had thrown a quill pen into his left facial cheek. Unbelievably, the point of the pen stuck in him like a dart in a dartboard, and the entire general science class roared with delight.

But Mort received two stiches and a serious infection from that one, and, more seriously, he had lost two days of work. That was $80, half a month's rent. Mira demanded Mort's share of the rent the last day of each month, and Mort had difficulty coming up with the $160 because the hospital bill had to be paid—he had no medical insurance—and it came to $120. So after he had paid Mira, he had $12 to eat on. He was tempted to go live with his mother and father again, but they had said a final goodbye to him and he knew it. He was the youngest of nine children, and his mother and father were already making plans to move to Tampa-St. Pete when his father retired in June. So his presence would not be desired at home. He would have to eat peanut butter and Rice Krispies for a week and a half.

And he did.

He ate his lunches at McDonald's when he had the money. He alternated between the Big Macs, the Quarterpounders, the fish sandwiches, the cheeseburgers, and all the remaining entrees. He liked to think there was some variety in his life.

Whenever he worked on the southwest side, as he was today, he enjoyed going to the McDonald's on 79th and Western. There was a blonde, (but Jewish-looking) girl who always worked on weekdays. Inevitably, Mort stood in her line to have her wait on him. He thrilled to the way she stuffed his lunch bag. He delighted in watching her draw draughts of his Diet Seven-Up. There was something erotic and glamorous about this tall, small-breasted lithe of a girl.

She paid no attention to Mort; she probably figured he was simply another of those insignificant people who snarfs up burgers and swills soft drinks, Mort reasoned.

She didn't smile at him and wish him a good day, as she handed him his change. Mort lowered his head just slightly—he didn't want her to see it—and he made his way back to a littered table and he sat down to eat his melted-cheese-fish-burger. There was too much mayonnaise and relish on it and he thought about taking it back, but he didn't want to chance making the blonde, Jewish-looking teenager mad at him. So he ate in silence while a mother and her six noisy, highly obnoxious young boys tried to break his concentration on his fish-burger and Diet Seven-Up. But they didn't swerve him from his lunch. He was resolute.

He chewed on.

The bad time came in the first class after the lunch break. They were still freshman boys, but some of these people, Mort figured, must have been Merchant Marine dropouts. There was a black kid in the third row who was well over six feet tall (all of them appeared to be taller than their substitute) and he had a scar that ran from his left temple to the cleft on the right side of his chin. It was purple and hideous, Mort thought. It must have been received in a knife fight. It was too gruesome-looking to be a birthmark or to be the delineation of some accident. He looked like a *bad mother* to Mort Klein. They all did. So he began to feel the tremors of fear that accompany the magisterial feeling which is known as lack of control.

He could handle insults. (He was called a twisted-faced-*white-mother* on the steps of Alonzo Jones High School.) He had been threatened at least a half dozen times on his way to his 1963 white, four-doored Rambler after school had let out. And there was of course the time that brute landed his quill harpoon in Mort's left cheek.

Lack of control was the ultimate horror-show. There would be disruptive behavior, just the way he was taught there would be in Educational Psychology. He could handle individual cases of that. What he feared was an all-class attack upon him. He feared mob action, when there is a leader involved, and when that leader incites even the most passive of acneeds into open revolt. Mort had heard of cases of such wars in the various faculty lounges of the schools where he had substituted. But he tried not to believe any of those tales. He wouldn't allow himself to believe.

"But what if they did?" he pondered.

Just as suddenly as Mort suspected the large black boy of being the ringleader of a revolt, just that suddenly the large, scarred Negro began to write out the busy-work that Mort had, with great trepidation, turned his back to the class and written on the chalkboard. The black kid never mumbled, cursed, or displayed any sign of aversion to keeping his mouth shut for the hour and completing the work Mort had chalked on the board.

Mort almost breathed out noticeably, but he let his breath out slowly, and no one heard the sound of terror hissing out of his lips.

Mort had made only one other resolution after he got out of the hospital in January. He resolved that he would never go into another classroom without what he called 'the edge.'

Mort smiled when he thought about his 'edge.' His leverage over them. He was thankful that he didn't have to use his 'edge' against them. It was far more effective than calling a dean or a principal into a classroom, and it was sure to catch their short attention spans hurriedly.

Mort had never had call to use his edge since he was released from the hospital in January, but he knew he would resort to it if it meant protecting himself from physical harm. He wasn't going to allow any punk to stick anything sharp into his body again. He wasn't going to tolerate anyone physically molesting him. That was for sure.

Because $40 a day certainly wasn't worth dying for. He was more significant than that. He had told Mira so, but she hadn't paid much attention to him when he had told her, last week. She had been busy preparing her bedroom for another of her gentile visitors. (He asked her if she ever had anything to do with Jews other than himself, and she had answered that she wasn't having anyting to do with him, and so she didn't know what the hell he was talking about.)

The surprise was inside his brown, torn briefcase. It had been his father's briefcase back when his father had still been an electrical engineer. (His father was now in supervision, a significant job.) Mort had picked it out of the trash because his mother didn't believe in hanging onto the old. She believed in the consuming of goods, just like in *Brave New World*.

Mira didn't love him and couldn't, she had said. He couldn't move back with his parents, and he wouldn't. And the blonde girl at the McDonald's at 79th and Western wouldn't pay attention to him, and she didn't. So those were some of the additional reasons that Mort carried his 'edge' in his father's old, torn, and discarded briefcase.

The huge black teenager worked steadily at his busy work for the entire hour. The rumble of discontent and the undercurrent of rowdiness had died a quick death. He was amazed. It became so quiet that he was able to take out his thick paperback copy of Bertrand Russell's *A History of Western Philosophy*. He was halfway through the section on the Greek philosophers. He hoped he would be up to the Catholic philosophers by the end of spring. Reading about Nietzche and Hegel and all the rest was something for the future.

He smiled quickly. They didn't notice. It was five minutes to the bell, and they were hurriedly finishing up. Mort could see a single bead of perspiration on the scarred black's upper lip. Mort quickly grinned again. And this time nobody caught it, either. He shoved his brown briefcase a bit farther away from his chair with his right toe. He figured it wouldn't be necessary, today, to use his leverage.

But he was wrong. The last class of the day openly refused to begin the assignment. They were sullen about it, at first. A white boy in the first chair in the second row was mumbling obscenities under his breath, but Mort could not clearly make out what he was saying.

"What did you say?" Mort finally uttered.

"Huh?" the kid groaned.

They roared with laughter and approval.

"I said, what did you say to me?"

"I wasn't talkin' to you, pal," he spit.

Fourteen or fifteen years old, and he talked like a steel worker already, Mort thought.

"Don't call me pal, friend," Mort hissed, trying to sound paternalistically angry.

"I ain't yer friend."

"You better go see the dean. Right now."

"What fer?"

"Leave. Or I'll give you a gross misconduct."

"Shit," the boy whispered as he rose from the metallic shop table. "Yer only a goddam substitute!"

Again the classroom exploded with noise.

Mort edged his brown briefcase back next to his right calf.

"No. You just sit back down. I think you might as well stay right here."

"Huh?"

They giggled nervously with him. They were watching Mort. There were twenty-four of them in his class, most of them white, and all of them were dressed very shabbily. He was dealing with children of the lower middle class, just like this slightly-pimpled adolescent who was slowly sitting back down in his chair. Mort almost felt a twang of remorse for giving the obscene-mouthed boy a bad time. He wondered how many years away from the steel mills and the southwest side saloons this boy really was. He felt some kind of electric sadness for the boy.

But it passed swiftly because he remembered the kid was a threat to his control.

"No," Mort continued. "You just stay with us. Besides, I want to show you all something."

He reached down for his bag, and the room became silent.

"I think I better get to the dean. I know I did somethin' wrong an' I—"

"Sit down!" Mort breathed. And the coldness of his inflection startled Mort, himself.

"I said I wanted to show you people something."

"You gonna whip out yer wanger on us?" a voice boomed from the back.

They shrieked, and shivers shot up Mort's spine as he reached for the clasps of his briefcase.

"He ain't got nothin' to expose, the sheenee!" came bellowing from the opposite corner of the shop.

He laid it on the desk.

"Is that thing loaded?" the foul-mouthed boy asked.

"Sure," Mort assured him.

"Whatchyou want to have a gun fer? Yer a—"

"Oh, I just call it, I just call it my *babysitter*. It's like a pacifier. When the baby gets out of control, I just take out this pacifier. It seems to work."

Mort had never exposed his .38 police special before, so he was lying. But they would never know that. He had only bought it last February, on the day after Washington's birthday. And he had never been tempted to draw it out of its resting place before, but when that boy said he was only a substitute, something had cracked and broken inside him, like stomped-upon brush.

"Don't you wanna put that thing away?" the bad-mouthed kid pleaded.

"Oh no. I like it right here. In fact, I was thinking of giving you all a demonstration."

Mort looked up at the six globes of light. It was an old school and they hadn't gone to fluorescent light yet.

He pointed the pistol at the farthest left hand side globe. The boys at the table underneath the light hit the floor with a thud.

There was a general holding of breaths. Even Mort was shocked that he had pointed the pistol at anything. He had only destroyed a few beer bottles and cans with the gun out in the forest preserves on cold days when no one was around to get hurt or to hear him do the shooting.

"I'm a good shot. Don't worry. If you'll all get under the tables. Right now! Go ahead."

He heard them plopping and smacking aginst the green tile. He could only see the green between piles of unswept sawdust.

"That's right. Now close your eyes and put your faces to the floor."

He was amazed by his self-control, and by his control over them. There were twenty-four boys struggling impossibly to get each of their bodies totally beneath the metal shop tables. It was impossible, of course. Some of their limbs stuck out into the aisles.

"Let's tuck those arms and legs in, in the back there. I certainly wouldn't want to injure anyone."

"Christ, he's crazy!" someone bleated from the middle of the floor.

"Nooo, this is just a demonstration. Something you learned at school today. And do you know what you're learning in woodshop today? Do you?"

No one was foolish enough to answer. They knew that most of their bodies were exposed from beneath the shop tables.

"You are learning respect for persons! That's what you're learning! Everybody counts! Do you hear?"

No one answered, as before. It was fifteen minutes before the bell. And the woodshop was located next to the gymnasium, and the gym and shop were in a separate wing of the old high school. There were no gym classes going on at the moment, and the male gym instructor was taking his coffee at the teachers' lounge in the adjoining wing of the building. So nobody could hear; nobody could witness Mort's demonstration.

"You are learning to be aware of the fact that all human beings are worthy, they are each important. They are all valid statements of, of the existence of God!"

A boy was beginning to weep, on the left-center of the floor.

"Don't do that! I'm not going to hurt you. I'm not a homocidal maniac! This is simply a demonstration! Don't you all see?"

The same boy was down to a whispering-gurgling, now.

"This is simply for your education, for your personal, educational benefit. When I walked in here, none of you thought I was worthy of your attention. Did you? 'He's only a substitute,' you thought. Didn't you? But you didn't know."

Mort looked at the gun, and he knew why they were quiet. He felt the surge of his control, his power, ebbing. He knew he couldn't keep them under the tables much longer. Soon the gym teacher would be back, and soon the bell would ring.

"You don't have any idea how sad this all is. You'll probably think it's very funny, when you leave."

They were still stonily silent.

There were six minutes remaining until the bell. The gym teacher would be returning sooner than that.

Mort thought of Mira. He knew he didn't love her. He had enjoyed sleeping with her until he had found out that the love making was for her a simple and casual release. Mort thought that intimacy had to be—it had to be significant, too. You just didn't do it with anybody.

He would pack and he would leave her. He had a full tank of gas in the Rambler and it got great mileage, too. He had a cousin in New York who was always asking him to come out and stay with him. And his cousin, Mark, lived on a farm. Mark was a lawyer, and he practiced law in the small towns that surrounded his land. He picked weeds and defended chicken thieves, Mark used to joke. Mort could be halfway to upstate New York by late tonight if he got the hell out of here before the bell rang and the gym teacher arrived.

His mother and father could be told about his move later. They were busy planning their move to Tampa-St. Pete. And the girl at the McDonald's at 79th and Western? Well, they would have country blondes waiting on him in upstate New York. Maybe Mark could help him get a job. He had had it with teaching, and even if he were offered a fulltime position, he was through with the classroom. Maybe he could pick weeds and spread manure for Mark. Perhaps he could learn to be a legal assistant. There was a chance he could find work. There had to be work up there, he was sure. He didn't have to stay here.

"I'll bet dat thing ain't even loaded," someone hoarsely whispered from the back.

There was a stirring of bodies and a titter of gathering laughter.

Mort smiled. He cocked the pistol and pulled the trigger and first there was a WHAMPPP from the discharge and then there was a PWOPPPP!! as the left rear light globe exploded.

There was a muffled shriek from a few of the boys under the front tables.

Mort grinned. He was a shade under five feet six inches tall, and the best you could say of him and his physique was 'wiry.' But he knew they were aware of his existence now, and he didn't care that the gun was the catalyst of their fear of him.

He squeezed off five more quick shots, he demolished each of the remaining five globes with staccato PWOPPPS! and harsh CRACKS! from his pistol, and as the glass shattered, fell, and sprayed about the floor, he could see the boys clutching their unguarded limbs in close to the trunks of their bodies.

There were two minutes left until the bell. The gym teacher was late returning to his gym.

"I'm reloading," he giggled. "I hope you've all learned something today."

Now he smiled broadly, showing his straight, only slightly yellowed teeth. He was small of stature, yes, he thought, but he was somewhat attractive, in a wiry way.

He stuck the .38 police special back into his torn, tan briefcase. He put *A History of Western Philosophy* back into his satchel as well.

"Goodbye, gentlemen."

As he walked past the still-huddled-upon-the-floor boys, down the center aisle, he heard his heels crunching the delicate glass of the shattered lights. He could smell the acrid stench of the gunpowder, but it wasn't offensive.

Before he walked out the door, toward his Rambler and his cousin, Mark, and toward New York and a job as a weed-puller and legal assistant, he turned to the still-face-down, clutching boys and said:

"You tell your regular teacher that you behaved perfectly for the substitute today. Do you hear?"

He bolted abruptly from the classroom, sprinted toward the exit door with his key to the Rambler clutched in one hand and the beaten-up leather handle of his once-discarded briefcase clutched solidly in the other, and he beat it in a hurry toward his waiting white box of an automobile.

ALBUM

If we leave by midnight we can make it to Georgia by mid-morning, I think. I haven't been south since college. Thank God we're not going to Daytona. What a hell hole. Kids just swarming all over the beach, the motels, and the restaurants. It's no vacation in Daytona. Just another Frankie Avalon, Annette Whatsername beach spectacular. Except the real goings on, on the beach, are a bit more maudlin.

The only state I can remember that was at all scenic was Tennessee. Maybe that's because you pass through the unscenic parts of Kentucky and Georgia on the way down.

With Freddy at the wheel, I'm sure we won't take any alternate routes in order to catch the beauty of the countryside. He'll want to make an almost straight line for southern Florida and the Keys.

You'd think July would be an awfully hot month to go to the Keys. I think we should go to Cape Cod, or even to Montreal. But he says his aunt and uncle'll put us up for a night in Florida. And that's $30 we won't have to spend on a motel and meals.

My dress feels awfully close. The air conditioning at St. Theresa's is not working too swiftly. I'm sweating. My mother's sweating. And my sister Jill's down to the nub of her last fingernail. Her right pinky. "What're you so nervous about?" I tease. She smiles widely, and out pops a fragment of a soggy fingernail. Out onto the red carpet. "Jill, you're a little animal. Quit chewing," I say. She keeps right on chewing.

As if she was about to embark on her holy maiden voyage. She's only fifteen. And she believes everything she reads in *Cosmo* and *Mademoiselle* and all the others. Especially all the stuff about the beauties and joys of modern sexuality. She considers herself very liberated, already. God, she just can't wait to talk things over with her husband. Things like 'how can I better please you, and how can you better please me?' If Mom ever finds out what she's been up to since she was fourteen, little Jill will be on a leash, in the basement. She's on the pill already. The doctor wanted to do something about her menstrual problems, but he merely opened the door for darling Jill. And like some very big-time, fully grown adult, she talks about-'discusses' her monthly bloating and all that tremendously important grown-up woman stuff, with me.

I refuse to take the pill. I refuse to puff up like a water buffalo when Freddy could take precautions, just as well as I.

But I'm weakening. I think eventually that I'll have to go to them. We really don't want a child for a few years. And we both don't like the worry and the hassle and the incompleteness and all that.

One thing is, I certainly didn't start off as early as sis, here. I was seventeen when I first made love. And I was pretty damned particular about my partner. I made sure he had nice tight lips is what I made sure of.

Jill tells me everything. I'm her numero uno confidante. She tells me how 'X' kisses with his mouth too wide open and how he clacks teeth with her; and how 'Y' insists on attacking her at the beach in the water and how he always falls asleep at the drive-in (she calls it a water fetish).

My sister's a weirdo. A jerk.

I love her.

Freddy kisses me with his eyes open. And every time I catch him at it, we both start laughing. It invariably destroys the mood.

He's very consistent in his ideas about sex. He's told me, right out loud:

"I like sex to be dirty and sneaky and sweaty and in the bedroom where nobody in the rest of the goddam world can see what you're doing."

He's a romantic prince, he is.

I want the reception to be at least slightly dignified. I think I'll tell the bartenders to keep the drinks a little watery. I don't want any fights, any weeping or wailing. And, God, I don't want his buddy, Falcone, to get grabby. Falcone is a notorious fanny grabber. I refuse to let him ruin our wedding.

And my mother gets silly when she drinks, too. She becomes a bit too romantic with my father, when she feels a little high. She kisses and squeezes him until he has to get up and retreat to the john, in an awful, embarrassed rage. Then, when he's gone, she slobbers all over her sisters about how she's got a prince among men for a husband. And they get sick and I get sick and my mother never believes the way she acts, when I tell her the next day.

He will not be drinking this night. I'm going to keep him away from Falcone and the rest of his little friends and cronies. Even if I have to drag him around the dance floor the entire time.

When he gets smashed, he likes to join in the festivities with his little friends from Garvey's. They play a cute game called "Take a bow." You hear these fully grown morons telling each other, "Take a bow" (when they're good and schnockered) and then you see one of them doubling over in pain. You see, "Take a bow" is a prelude for one of these lucky children. A prelude to kneeing the other darling fellow in the groin. They think it's all absolutely hilarious.

How can you deal with people like that? Alfred's drinking Bubble-Up tonight, that's how.

I wonder how she felt right before she married my father. Was she nervous, or was she too busy to be bothered? Did she think about what she was really doing? I mean making the final move and all.

Final is a strange word to use these days, isn't it? Divorce is as easy as falling out of bed. There's nothing final about marriage any more. Not necessarily, anyway.

At least divorce allows room for error. Unless you're a Catholic, like I am, and unless you want to remarry and remain a Catholic.

There's something mighty cruel going on there. It's cruel and I don't give a damn about canon law.

I'm lucky my father can't hear all of that.

I hope I never have to worry about it with Freddy. I want us to work, of course. And I want us to beat all those odds and statistics. I want to live a very corny, average, predictable, uneventful, happy life with him.

I don't care about the places I'll never see, the other men I'll never meet, the vacations by myself that I'll never be able to take. I'm sure about what I'm doing. I'm sure that I'm sure.

The sound of my own voice, huh?

"Quit chewing those damned fingernails!"

She jumps up, surprised.

Did you ever sit down and list the reasons why you love someone? Sounds ridiculous, doesn't it? I haven't actually sat down and written a list on a piece of paper, but I can almost describe the things that are lovable about him by rote:

He's romantic. He cries at the end of *Lassie Come Home.* Every time. He believes the best about people until there's just no doubt that the person's a stinker. Nixon was a bad scene for Freddy. And he voted for McGovern.

He loves westerns. He thinks James Arness is a god, for God's sake. He likes movies where the good guy gets crapped on by the bad guy for an hour and forty five minutes, and then, when the bad guy's at the mercy of the hero at the end, the lead, in a burst of superiority, lets the villain crawl off in the dust. I mean the good guy could've killed the sucker, but he lets him go. You know?

He's loyal to the people he loves. I'm positive he hasn't gone out on me. Mainly because we see each other just about every day. And he's extremely possessive of me, too. I know I could crush him so very easily, if I wanted to.

He's affectionate. It's obvious when he's with me that that's true. I remember once, while we were driving to his parents', he ran down a squirrel. And unfortunately the squirrel didn't die immediately after being hit. Freddy stopped the car and got out and almost picked up the bloody, furry little thing in his hands. But he stopped short. He came back to the car and told me to close my eyes. He said he was going to run the animal over again, and put it out of its misery. So I closed my eyes and waited. When I felt that we were not moving, I opened my eyes and saw him looking over the steering wheel at the struggling squirrel. He couldn't press his foot to that pedal. His eyes were actually filling with tears. The car wasn't moving, his foot was frozen, and he was ready to cry out loud. And then I saw that the creature had stopped its jerking and writhing. It was dead. Freddy couldn't move. I had to drive the rest of the way.

And he's in love with me! He wants to be with me for a long, long time, he says. He wants my children. He wants to get old with me. Absolutely corny and obvious, isn't he?

I absolutely love him.

II

Just once, if somebody stood up and gave a reason why the two of us should not be joined together in marriage, I think I'd upchuck and die. I mean really die. That's the kind of nightmare you have, about two weeks running, every night, before the wedding.

In my dream we're at the United Nations, and they're in session. Everybody is voting on something and I'm standing in the middle of everything all alone on a sort of a platform and I can see them standing about the room yelling into their microphones, "Nyet! No! Nay!" and I see a fat bald guy pounding on his lectern with his shoe, a tan pennyloafer, and he's screaming, "Nah, Nah Nah, Nah NAH NAHHHHHHH!!!" like a ten year old and then, suddenly, dolphins come swimming into the room, but there's no water, and they're still swimming into the room and Freddy's riding the lead dolphin, like a cowboy in his saddle and he's digging his spurs into the side of the porpoise and the gray and white animal's bleeding and I'm screaming at Freddy telling him to stop hurting the dolphin and I run up to him and drag him off the suspended-in-air beast and as he thumps on the ground I see blood on the front of my white bridal gown just like in *Hush Hush Sweet Charlotte* and I'm screaming and shrieking and Freddy's laughing and saying, "It's only a joke, baby, only a joke," and the rest of the delegates in the room are thundering, "No! Nay! Nyet! No! No!" and I'm crying, "You don't have a good reason! You don't have a good reason! You don't have a good reason!"

And then I usually wake up and find my covers and pillow thrown all over the floor.

When the priest asks me if "I do", I almost hesitate and turn and look around the room. But I don't. I lock my face forward and without a pause, I smile and say, "I do."

There wasn't much wrong with the ceremony, other than the fact that I came too close to a candle and almost caught my veil on fire. As soon as I saw that flame brushing close to me, a picture of Freddy bending over a charred pile of woman and blackened remnants of veil and gown shot into my brain. I could see him fingering through the debris, wailing, "Dee Dee, Dee Dee, where are you, my darling?" I almost laughed out loud, but Freddy was kissing me and we were turning around and smiling at aisles full of gleaming faces and the sunlight was peeking melodramatically through the stained glass windows at the back of the church. The light was glaring off the floor of the middle aisle. I had to blink.

III

My father insisted on Nelson's Nordic Restaurant for the reception. It had to be class and expensive, and he refused to offer his guests a plate with a diddly piece of roast beef and a scoop of mashed potatoes and a fruit cocktail cup. So he rented a smorgasbord place. And he's supplying the booze himself. He told me he's giving the bartenders an extra $10 apiece if they make the drinks *major league.*

That's thrilling. I can just see 250 sick people staggering out of here around midnight. And after I told him that I wanted some semblance of calm at this reception.

The band is a typical you-don't-dance-till-you're-drunk combo. I'll bet their favorite number is "The Bunny Hop." I can't wait.

The head table is set beautifully, I have to admit. In fact, the entire place is rather swank. I suppose I know that weddings are for the guests, not for the two marrieds. Just like funerals, marriage is a ritual. A reason to celebrate. And everybody knows more people are dying every day than are getting married, so I think I'll relax and let them have their good time.

Freddy is absolutely beautiful in his black velvet tux. I've never seen him so happy looking. I hope it's because of us and not because his fraternity brothers and he are getting one helluva free drunk. He's not taking a bite out of the apple until we reach Macon,

Georgia, at the Holiday Inn. With me, in bed, where a husband belongs.

He's a handsome devil, I gotta say. He has dark brown, wavey (almost curly) hair and the weirdest green-brown eyes you've ever seen. There are little specks of green laid almost geometrically on a background of brown. No matter what his facial expression may be, when you look into his eyes it's like looking into a cat's eyes. Almost like an *evil eye*, but a lot more kindly and a lot more hypnotic.

And he's got muscular, big hams for forearms. He's a bit flabby around the middle, but he's solid as an oak. I mean you could bounce off him if you bumped into him. Freddy's 6' 1", I think. He weighs a bit over 200. He lacks only one thing. He has no fanny. (When we came back from a purple passion party once, and were on our way into Freddy's house, I remembered I'd left something in the car. He told me that he'd leave the front door open. God, he was smashed. That rotten grape juice and grain alcohol. Anyway, when I got to the front door, I found his pants lying on the doorstep. And the belt was still buckled. After he wandered out of the john, he looked at the trousers and grinned. "I sneezed," he said. And then I looked down at those pants again, and back up at his flat backside, and I began to laugh like an idiot. He was blushing like the most crimson cardinal you've ever seen.)

He grips your hand like an axe handle, for God's sake. When he playfully squeezes your arms, you hemorrhage and have black marks for two weeks. His fingers are stubby and look like ten blunt instruments (if you include thumbs with 'fingers'. His thumbs are crooked. He broke them in some damned softball game; one was broken by a line drive, and the other was broken when he fell down from the shock of breaking the first one.) But, when he touches my face with his fingertips, it's like a breeze suddenly popping in from your west window, tickling your nose and ears and cheeks.

His mother is small and looks younger than she is. In fact, she's in fabulous shape for a woman of 63 years. About 5'4", and I'll bet she only weighs about 125. That's fantastic for a woman her age. She's always ragging at Freddy about his weight, but she's a very kind person. And she's held together like a trooper after Freddy's dad, Martin, died two months ago. It kills Freddy, it absolutely kills him, that his dad didn't live to see this day. His only son getting married, and cancer kills him two months before the wedding.

Well, enough.

My mother's a bit more stout than Freddy's mom. She's taller, too. And my dad's about 6'3" and skinny as a shoe string. One of those ungodly high metabolism people. Eats like a wanton razorback and never gains a pound.

They're both good Catholics. Lots of my father's money goes to St. Theresa's every Sunday. All his kids, Jill and I and Randy (my older brother), went to parochial grade and high schools. In fact he wanted badly for Randy to become a priest. But Randy's not here today. He's in Madison, Wisconsin, working on his doctoral thesis in sociology.

Freddy doesn't like Randy. They almost had it out at one of my parents' blowouts after Randy drunkenly called Freddy a Romantic Neanderthal. God, Freddy became enraged. That's the one time Gene Falcone has ever done anything for anybody. He broke it up; he took Freddy outside and calmed him down. But not before Freddy screamed back at Randy, "And what are you, you broken-down bone-picking college punk? Huh? What the hell are you?"

The meal is ready at about 6:30. There's roast beef and chicken and mashed potatoes and cole slaw and Jello and corn and peas and —my God, they have two entire tables filled with food. Stacks of beef and poultry and vegetables and desserts.

Freddy's mother takes a tablespoon of Jello, a single slice of beef, and a tablespoon of cottage cheese. And that's it. I look at my mound of calories and I become self-conscious. So, I look at Freddy (whose plate is equally as mountainous) and I place another breast of chicken on my plate. For some reason, I think I'm getting even.

I mean I'm not all that much overweight. Maybe three or four pounds. But I'm 5'7" and I hold most of my weight in my legs. I weigh about 133.

People are laughing and sipping bourbon and scotch and gin and vodka in the food line. Mom and Dad are busier telling their guests to stock up on food than they are filling up their own plates.

My father and mother are at their personal zeniths when they're handing out something to other people. Like Christmas. She'll give him a shirt and he'll give her an electric can opener, and they'll both spend about $500 on the three of us. You've never seen such pleasure in two faces as you see in theirs when Randy, Jill and I play grabbag in December. That's why my father's got about $200 in his savings account.

Before the meal begins, the best man, Gene Falcone, has to make a short speech. I'm not too concerned about it. He can't grope anybody from the speaker's podium, can he?

"I'd like to propose a toast to our newly married couple here. I'd like to propose that they have many children, few fights, and a long, long life together. And I hope they wear out a couple hundred mattresses together. Salud!"

Father Roberts is thrilled to death with the speech. He almost chokes on a gulp of his champagne when he hears the word "mattresses."

The meal goes very quickly. Most of our guests don't go up for seconds and thirds. They don't want to overdo the gluttony bit. So they all retire to the bar around 7:30. And the lines there become very, very long, almost immediately, and they never seem to diminish. I'm glad now that my father slipped the poor bartenders that $10.

It's time for me to make those inevitable rounds.

"You look heavenly, dear. How much did your dress cost?... I'll bet you spent at least— And the liquor and the food must have cost your father at least—"

"Are you going to have a family right away? Well, if you do, look out for those children's photographers. They're all bloodsuckers. Take the pictures yourselves. You do want a boy, don't you?"

"And if the toaster doesn't work, make sure you bring it back. $17.50, for goodness sake. It better work. It's got a year guarantee."

"Where did you get your hair done? I didn't know that it was so naturally curly. Barbara's hair is beautifully straight. She can do anything with her hair that she wants. Blondes should have straight hair. It's so much more manageable. Don't you agree?"

Etc, etc, etc.

And where else would Freddy be? With Gene Falcone and Manny Bozsufo and Ray Delgado and Murray Maniates. The heart of Garvey's Come Back Inn. And the idiots are all drinking boilermakers. Immediately I inform my husband that we're expected on the dance floor. Like a little boy who's been caught in the refrigerator, I take him by the hand and lead him to the middle of the floor.

God only knows what they're playing, with their saxophone, accordion, trumpet, bass, piano, and drums. But it sounds like a two-step, and we're suddenly alone on the dance floor.

I smile and hear my dress swishing against the tiles. And Freddy is smiling at me, in his cat-eyed, semi-grimaced way.

I'm a Russian countess for almost a minute and forty-five seconds. For one tiny fragment of my life, I'm an empress. I'm Anastasia come home to Petersburg and I can pretend that he's bald and that he speaks with a slight Slavic accent. The floor is empty, and there is a large circle of faces around us. I can look up at the ceiling and see gigantic crystalline chandeliers hanging from and pocking the accoustic tile above us. He is wearing a monocle now, and a red sash stretches from his right shoulder to his left hip. The music is carrying us. I can hear violins and cellos and stringed basses and the music is Strauss. The accordion is not creaking, the bass is not thumping, the trumpet is not honking. The music is Strauss and we're waltzing across the diamond, glistening room and our feet are not clomping, they're floating about the floor. He is holding me erect with his hand near the base of my back. He is holding me on the ground, keeping me from rising like helium.

He dances soundlessly and smoothly. I feel him taking command of the music. The music is keeping tempo with him. And here am I, keeping up with him and the music.

And the helium, the lightness in my head, evaporates to the familiarity of "Moon River" and Henry Mancini and the creaking of the accordion and the shrill beer-commercial-tinkling of the piano.

I can see my mother and father standing in an absolute beam of sunlight, at the inner edge of the circle. I motion to them all like a happily drowning Ahab, and many of them join us on the dance floor.

I put my face on his right shoulder and my right cheek touches his. He knows that the waltz is nearly over and that I'm asking him to hold me close. He holds me a bit tighter, with his right arm, and I want to leave the hall right now and be half way to Georgia. I want to sit next to him and count the miles and kiss his ear and neck and listen to a sleepwalking all night radio show and get groggy and sentimental and arouse him just a little so that he'll be anxious like I am.

We'll stop at a hamburger stand, an all night place, in Indiana or Kentucky, and the onions and the meat will taste like sirloin and mushrooms at 3:00 A.M. And the business of travelling will be romantic, as it always is, for me.

When my cousins came in from Boston a few years ago, I remember them leaving, after a week's stay with us. They were all packed and bundled into their station wagon, and my two cousins were stretched out in sleeping bags in the back. I would have given my father anything if he would have let me go with them. Watching the night sky and the headlights behind us and stopping at gas stations in a sleepy stupor and hearing the clink clink clink of the gas pump and the squishing of the squeegee across the windows and then the road and the night air as it comes wafting in across your face and rising sweetly into your nose. And you're always moving. There's always another place to head toward. Another 250 or 150 or 50 miles to go. You never quite arrive. There's only movement and the smell of hamburger from ten miles down the road.

We're scheduled to leave here at about 10:30. We've got to get around to everybody, everbody who's still sober enough to say goodbye. We've got to thank them all and pack up all those boxes and packages and envelopes and somehow get on the road before midnight or one.

There is a table filled with gifts, thin and rectangular boxes and fat and square boxes. And there seems to be more than a hundred envelopes. Freddy is happy to see the envelopes because they mean cash.

"If they give us cash we can buy our own bath towels and our own china and our own goddam service-for-eight. I hope they keep their goddam salad bowls and hand us over some green currency."

He gets his wish.

Freddy and Gene and Manny make at least ten trips to our car (a 1971 Pontiac that I hope he's going to trade in before it blows up. God, I hope we make it back before it goes poof). They're both (Gene and Manny) staggering out and in continuously, and I'm pleased that my husband is shepherding them to and from the car in a sober, benevolent manner.

When we're finally ready and packed up, and when we've both changed clothes, we try to find our parents. And we find the three of them sitting at the head table. The white table cloth is covered with crumbs and stains and wrinkled up, dirty red napkins. My father is tired, I can tell. He is holding a Seven-Seven in his right hand and I can see that the glass is no longer sweating and that there are no ice cubes left in the drink. In another minute he'll be asleep with his eyes open.

But the women are still talking and carving the air with their hands (my mother is doing most of the talking and gesticulating) until Freddy and I come over to them and say that we're ready to get started.

My father suddenly comes out of his glazed stupor and mumbles, "Oh, oh, oh." He reaches out for Freddy's hand and tells him to take care of his little girl and to give her a good life and to be happy and to have a good time in the sun because it's been so wet here lately, and to be careful on the road with all those hillbillies in Indiana and Kentucky and Georgia and—

And he goes on and on about taking care of me and I'm thinking about all the years my father took care of me and I'm wondering again about my mother and the way she was 34 years ago. About how she was going to walk out of her reception hall and how she was going to start something all her own.

I mean if you look past all the obvious stuff about loving somebody and wanting to be with them, the real mystique about marriage is the adventure bit. It's something new. I mean people constantly jabber about not being ready for marriage, so there must be something you have to prepare for, if you see what I mean. Like before a trip or a voyage. And it must be pretty scary if people have to do all that soul searching before they embark on this journey.

Maybe that's an awfully romantic way of looking at it. But look, if you're 21 or 22, people look at you hesitantly and then ask you why you're not married already. So you get married so that you won't get any more of those jerky hesitant stares.

I don't know why marriages have become a shakey property and why divorce has become big business.

Maybe it's all this crap about living together and preparing yourself for natural changes in attitudes.

I don't know why it's taking so long to say goodby to them.

My mother is crying, of course, and my father has his arm around her, and Freddy's mother is struggling to compose herself. I guess there's nobody here to put their arm around her. My father's laughing and telling my mother that it's all right. But she's just a little bit drunk and she's sobbing and making me cry now, too. I kiss the three of them goodby.

IV

The traffic, even at 11:30, doesn't clear away until we're almost inside Indiana. The rain that started to fall right after the reception began has stopped. The sky is clearing, and when we get away from the city street lights and out onto the four lane highway, we can see the constellations clearly.

I look at him and he's concentrating on the highway. I can see flashes of green and white and yellow and amber striping his face as we drive past all the intersections and as we pass out into the open country of Indiana.

I've got him so perfectly pegged, don't I? I know what tickles him and I avoid sure-fire annoyances when I talk to him. I know that I'm better educated, so I don't come on with any intellectual jargon toward him. I even make more money than he does. But I'm not going to push him back to school. I'm not going to threaten him. I want us to last. I'm going to beat all those big numbers. I'm not in a dream world, I know we're going to have bad, dark times and I know I'm going to wonder if I love him any more and I'm going to wonder if there's somebody else who's—

I'm even going to go on the pill, to please him. And I'm never going to hang sex over his head as a means toward compromise. We'll stick to the argument. If he thinks I paid too much for sirloin, we're only going to argue about the price of meat, for God's sake.

I'll love him. I'll make him feel big, important. He'll be the one to come up with all our decisions (whether I know better or not) because I know that's the way things have to be for Freddy to work. You can call it macho, if you want to, but if dominant's the way he wants to feel, then dominant's the illusion I'm going to create. Because nobody really makes decisions anyway. You and your entire chemistry have already made your decisions anyhow. Just like a quarter in a slot machine.

And I've married Freddy. I really couldn't have done anything else. And who knows or cares what's going to happen in a day or in a millenium. And who wants to?

Indianapolis. 168 miles. Counting. I wonder just how warm the Keys are going to be. I wonder if my father has my mother safely in bed yet. I wonder if they're sober enough to make love tonight.

And Freddy's mother. Is she awake and alone in bed wondering what she's going to do to make tomorrow pass? That really pains me to think about. We're going to spend time with her. We really are.

Indianapolis. 159 miles. I'm getting hungry already. All that dreaming about onions and hamburgers and the night air is working on me. I ask Freddy to stop, and he tells me he will, the very next chance he has. It's a little after 3:00 A.M.

I look at him for a long hard moment and he senses my scrutiny. He looks at me and smiles at me with his cat-eyes.

"What are you thinking about?" he asks.

The sun will be up in about three hours. I want to see it rise.

CHRONICLE

MORNING

I have to be up at dawn, she says.
There might be some trouble at the school and we're supposed to get there before the rest of the kids do.
She's just trying to make it easier for me to get back to normal, she keeps on saying. I understand her, I think. She doesn't need to draw me any pictures.
Dad leaves for work at 5:30. He works by the Wisconsin border, construction. Things have been going better for him since the weather's been so dry. Every day is a work day lately, for him. And I know he'd rather be out of the house than be around while all this has been happening. He's never backed off or anything. I don't mean he'd like to run out on Mom and me. It's just that the last time a photographer showed up at school, Dad got pissed and threw a fist into his lens. The lens and camera popped back into the photographer's face, and Mom said we almost had a lawsuit on our hands. Until Dad paid for a new camera.
But I think he would rather be at work pounding nails, watching walls go up, pouring concrete. Anything. I know I'd be relieved to get out of here before the dawn breaks, these days.
Mom leaves for her secretary job at 8:00, so she has plenty of time to drive me to school. She's been taking me a half hour before

the playground officially opens, ever since the word got out.

I had the dream again last night. Same dream as always. It's a vampire movie in my head, of course. The creature's a man and he comes after me, like vampires do in the movies. But when he wraps his arms around me, and just when I think I'm going to see those two blood-dripping fangs, out pops two needles. They pop right out of his gums as soon as he opens his mouth wide.

I know what the dream means. I don't need a shrink to explain them to me.

All my family talks about it as if it's one big tragedy. One huge mistake somebody made. It was supposed to be just a blood transfusion and I wind up the way I am now. There's the lawsuit against the hospital, and I suppose we've got a good chance of winning some money from them.

But who cares? It's not like the money'll pay for my college education, like my Dad says. And when he said it in front of me, he colored kind of quick and then he embarrassed me in front of Mom by hugging me, long and hard. I'm getting too old to be hugged by him. I just thank God he didn't do that in front of—

I was going to say in front of my friends, but since they've all gone away, I guess I don't have to worry about them being an audience to my father being carried away.

I did my crying and I'm done with it. My mom still cries. Usually she tries to lock herself in her bedroom or in the john so I won't hear her, but it doesn't happen as often anymore.

We went to the hospital for counseling, but the psychiatrist didn't help us out very much. It just seems like you can weep over something for just so long, and then you get numb. My mom hasn't arrived at numb yet, but I think I'm there. I think I'm already there.

I'm not able to watch much television in the mornings any longer. We have to leave too early, and most of the daybreak stuff is a little childish, I think. *The Count Duckulas* and all that little guy stuff. I still get a laugh out of *The Brady Bunch* and *Andy Griffith*, but I've seen them all too many times to be interested in turning on the tube before we leave for school.

"You ready, Jay?" Mom asks.

I show her my lunch sack. I've developed the habit of making my own lunch in spite of her bitching about how much she loves to make it for me.

I could barely hear her because I'm still plugged into my Walkman, listening to Van Halen's new cuts. I can't hack the radio in the morning because they mostly play little guy tunes. You know, Pebbles and Belinda Carlisle and all those other ten year old's heartthrobs. I think I passed Madonna and all that in sixth grade, last year. Heavy metal is where I'm at, at the moment. Even those old dudes, Led Zeppelin, beat the hell out of all that candy-assed rock for all those pre-pubies.

So I got a disease. The sun still comes up. Every day. Sure, sometimes I feel sick and I stay home from school. But the sickness passes pretty fast, and I'm usually only out one day, now that they can't keep me out permanently.

It took three months of lawyers and judges to get me back in the time after the principal met Mom and me out in front of the school's steps. Naturally all the TV guys and the news guys were there. It scared me a little, but not as much as my vampire dream does. The nightmare with the monster with the hypo-needle fangs, I mean.

But now I go to school, and sometimes I pay attention in class and sometimes I don't give a shit what anyone's saying, all day long. Sometimes I just listen because the day drags by too slowly if I don't. So I guess I'm learning stuff whether I feel like it or not.

Some of my teachers are sympathetic. They go out of their way to make me feel like I'm still part of everything. But we all know it's a big joke. A farce, you know. I'm not stupid, even though I was never an acer student. I know when I'm being what they call patronized. There are kids and adults who are scared shitless I'll give them what I've got, and there are other people at school who just don't want to be around me because they think I'm the product of some junkie and his junkie wife. They know my story by now. They know it was the fault of that hospital. But some people think what they want to think, so it's all our faults that I'm around to remind them of something real unpleasant. It's like I'm the Elephant Man, except I'm not ugly like he was.

Maybe the ugly is just on my insides, they think. Maybe that's good enough for them to stay the hell away from me. I don't really know what they think because I'm damned if I'll ask them what's going on inside their fevery little skulls.

"Are you ready, Jay?" she shouts.

I turn off my music, take off the headphones, and we're out the door.

NOON

No photographers today. I'm old news by now. I'm sort of tolerated, you might say. They don't come any closer than they have to, but they at least leave me alone.

There was some name-calling when I first came back to school, but some of those patronizing teachers put a stop to it.

Maybe I'm giving those teachers too much the bad review here, but it's hard for me to know who to trust. I trust my mother and father, but that's as far as it goes. There are only the three of us in the family, and all Mom's and Dad's family are on the East Coast, a thousand miles away. And I don't think they're all fired up about getting on a jet and coming here to comfort us in our time of need.

I look back at the front of the classroom. It's fourth hour. Social studies. We're doing the colonial period, which is very boring, to say the least. The teacher, Mrs. Rolinski, is not the problem. It just seems like government and all that taxation without representation stuff is very dead weight. I know it's the history of our country and I know what a special place this country's supposed to be, but—

Then she starts talking about how we were "ostracized" by the Brits when we started raising hell over here, and my ears zoom in on her words. She goes on about how one of the biggest things that marks the U.S. is that we did all that fighting and dying for one big reason: The right to be different. Man, that really strikes a hefty bass note inside my chest for some reason I'm not real sure about. But after she says that business about the right to be different, I'm following her every word. Right up until the bell rings.

Then the girl across the aisle from me pops her gum. But she doesn't smile back at me when I shoot her some grins.

The dumb cooz.

I eat lunch by myself, off in a corner of the cafeteria. No one had to tell me to sit off by myself, but I knew enough to do it on my own. I like to eat by myself, anyway. There's nothing more stupid looking than feeding your face. I even have to look away when my mother and father get a little string of juice flowing down to their chins. It almost makes me want to gag, but I've learned to watch my plate, when I'm here at school and when I'm home at the dinner table.

I usually leave half of my lunch in the bag lately. Only thing that tastes good is sweets. So I dump the sandwich I made for myself —Mom insists I eat meat and bread or cheese and bread— and I eat Twinkies or Ho-Ho's or whatever goo my mother buys for the lunches. I drink a can of Coke or Pepsi along with them because I can't get milk down anymore.

It's raining today, and that's the worst time for me. When it's clear I can go out into our little campus and sit by myself till it's time to go to the next class. But when they keep us indoors, it seems like a very long forty-five minute period.

There are people who would talk to me, I'm sure. There are a couple of do-gooders in every school, I bet. This place is no different. But the fact is I've run out of stuff to say to people and I think they've run out of little nothings to share with me, so I'll save us both the trouble.

Thank Christ the bell rings and I'm off to Science. Today we're talking about the Voyager and how we're going to get back into space after that bad thing that happened a couple years back.

I remember that bad thing. I saw it on TV, like most everybody else.

It happened before I went to the hospital. It was for a simple day-in, day-out, run-of-the-mill operation. I had my appendix taken out. I don't really remember the transfusion.

The operation was a success. It went perfectly. My stomach ache just disappeared.

Evening

Van Halen is on my plugged-in, personal jukebox again. The tune is "Black and Blue." I'd really like to see them when they come into town next summer, but I don't plan on anything, of course. My mom keeps talking about high school and college. Instead of making her feel bad I just tell her I want to join the Air Force and fly jets like Tom Cruise in *Top Gun* and so she has to remind me that Cruise was a Navy pilot and I argue that she's confusing that flick with *An*

Officer and a Gentleman and then I don't remember what branch Cruise was in and my mother starts crying. I tell her she's making me feel bad and she makes herself stop.

She's pretty good about the emotional stuff. She knows when to get out of my face when she feels it coming on, it looks like to me. I'd thank her for it, but that would start her off, probably.

My dad doesn't get watery-eyed. At least never in front of me. I've seen him get angry, very macho-pissed. Like with that picture-taking dude, like I said. But he never gets broken-up emotional.

He pays attention to me. I mean he talks to me and he takes me places on the weekends when he's not working overtime. But he works weekends a lot lately. Says he can't pass up the extra money. Not when it's in-season, like now. Winter's coming fast, and my dad thinks it's going to be snowy and cold, the reverse of the hot and dry the summer and the early fall have both been.

He tries as hard as he can and I don't hold it against him for not being around more. Because hell, the truth is he and Mom'll be around for a while yet. They gotta go on living. They ain't going anywhere for a while yet.

He walks into my bedroom, and I turn off the Walkman and take off the earphones.

"Van Halen again? Don't you ever get tired of that tape? I'll buy you some new ones Saturday."

"I like what I've got, Dad. Haven't got time to listen to the ones I already got from the record club."

He sits down on my bed.

"Want to go to a Cubs game this weekend? I don't have to work. New job doesn't start up for a week, and then I'll be at it until the snow flies."

"Sure. Fine."

He touches my hand lightly, but his hand doesn't linger.

"Mom'll be going, too. Got box seats. From a guy at the last job. Sold 'em to me for cost."

"Great."

He wants to ask me how I'm feeling, so I help him out.

"I'm O.K. Really. O.K., Dad."

"Lost any more—"

"A pound. Just one pound. It's the heat, like I already told you."

"Sure. The heat. It's been a bitch. Only good time, even with the air conditioning on, is when the sun's going down. Like now."

I look out the window next to my bed and I see he's right.

He turns on the lamp next to my bed then.

"Doctor, tomorrow," he reminds me.

"Why bother?"

"What do you mean, why—"

But he turns off his macho-pissed voice almost as quickly as he turned it on.

"They're going to cure this shit, Jay. You just gotta—"

"No, they're not. Not fast enough."

"There's stuff in the paper every—"

"It's crap, Dad. You know it and I do."

"The counselor told you that hope—"

"I let go of that a while ago."

He stands up. He looks down at me, not sure whether he should be angry or sympathetic. I see things crossing his face quicker than he can handle all that traffic.

"You have to hope, Jay. It's all there is to do."

I could put on my own macho-pissed face and tell him to go to hell, that he doesn't know, nobody knows except for me. It's my life, and it's my death, too.

But I don't argue.

"I hope. Sure. I hope."

I turn off the lamp and the redness of sunset creeps into my bedroom. He stands in the twilight-lit room with me for a long time, but he won't look at me.

"We'll make that game in the afternoon and then we'll take in a movie at one of those fancy suburban malls after we eat a nice dinner. Your mother loves to go out for dinner."

Now he finally turns to me, and he touches my hand lightly and quickly, once more. He leaves then, so I turn on my Van Halen tape and I plug back in.

I'm washed in the heavy metal. The guitars sound like violins and the organ and the bass and drums sound like the rest of an orchestra. I look out my window and I see the last red rays being swallowed by the horizon, and I turn up the volume. It sounds like a symphony. Like Beethoven gone nuts.

I'm remembering school and Mrs. Rolinski talking about our "right to dissent" and all that colonial stuff, and I forgive her and all the other teachers for being nice to me. I forgive our principal, Mr. Farnsworth, for not being so nice to me. I forgive all my classmates for letting me get away with sitting by myself at lunch. I forgive my mom for being a crybaby about all this, and I forgive my father for working all those weekends.

I even forgive the guy or woman who gave me the bogus needle at the hospital.

But I have trouble letting God off the hook for all my vampire dreams. I don't think they were really necessary.

I lied to my father about the weight loss. It was three pounds and not just one. And tomorrow the doctor'll make me stand on the scale and everyone'll know the truth.

I think the worst thing about being all alone is that it takes so long. If I got struck by lightning, it'd be over in a milli-second. But when you're alone you find yourself doing things like listening to even the most boring teachers, at school.

And I've started to listen to late-night radio at home. You know, those talk shows. Drunks call up and try to listen to themselves on the radio. They like to hear the sound of their own voices, I guess. They ask a lot of stupid crap and they say things that are dumber than hell.

But I suppose I forgive them, too. They're just like me, in a way. They don't want to go to sleep, and neither do I. I just don't want to say dumb things over the air and then have someone ask me the next day if it was me who said them.

It'll be a long night again tonight. It's not really one hundred percent dark out yet. The sun dies hard some nights.

I turn up my Van Halen tape. It's beating on my eardrums, but I don't care.

When the tape's over, I'll turn on one of those talk shows on AM. They come on around nine.

My mother'll come in here to give me the goodnight kiss about ten. And naturally she'll remind me about my doctor's appointment tomorrow. But she'll leave quickly because the word

'doctor' gets her teary, most of the time. She'll kiss me on the cheek twice and then she'll leave, and then I'll be alone again.
    I'll listen to the radio until I finally fall asleep.
    Late night radio does it to me every time.

BLUE COLLAR

Stanley Sliwa is the sweetest human being I know. But try to help him out and all you get is a stone wall and a heartache for your trouble.

He was divorced from his wife Marya five years ago, and he's kept the torch for the woman ever since. The divorce came about, we all thought, because of the death of their baby.

Actually the baby was never born. Marya fell down some icy stairs when she was in her eighth month, and the baby died from the injuries caused by her fall. Marya never blamed Stash, our Polish diminutive of Stanley, in public, nor did she ever accuse him of anything at home, in their privacy. But we all figure it was what was on her mind when she filed for the divorce. She was always a secretive, keep-it-hidden type woman. We liked her, but we all thought she was rather stange, too. Very artistic type. Played the piano. Danced ballet. Wrote poetry.

And Stash? He's the second shift foreman at the chemical plant my father used to work at. It's the plant I used to work at, before I became a teacher and a coach.

So the baby dies, Marya splits with Stash, Stash becomes broken-hearted and a recluse, and we don't see him for almost two years after the papers become final. Then we see him only rarely, after those two years of hiding out.

But he doesn't seem the same. You never met a more positive

human being than Stanley Sliwa before the tragedy, and after, after, he becomes somber, moody, the entire depressive route. Only he never talks about his feelings, about his depression. I have to sniff it out with my intuition, because you cannot get Stanley Sliwa to open up.

As I say, it's five years later, and the moment is a Thursday night at Garvin's Comeback Inn. I don't make it in here very often anymore because I've moved to the suburbs, and Berwyn is a little out of my way these days. But I come back here during softball season, and we've just blown a 8-7 game to the Cicero Pack-Rats, our arch-enemy. Garvin's brother-in-law owns the tavern in Cicero, so it's like an evening of mourning at the Comeback when Stanley Sliwa amazingly walks in at 9:00 P.M. I know the time because the Cubs game from San Diego is just coming on the tube.

He sees me sitting with Manske, our centerfielder, and Manny Bozsufo, another of our outfielders, and he comes over to me.

"Freddy."

"Stash. How are you?"

"O.K. Just O.K., I guess."

He sits down on my right. Bozsufo and Manske are in their own little world, commiserating about our fate to the Pack-Rats. So I've got Stash to myself.

"Where the hell have you been, Stanley?"

"You know. Busy."

"Busy doing what?"

He doesn't look up from his beer that Garv has just deposited in front of him.

"I've missed you for a long time, Stashu. You didn't have to go underground, you know."

Again he doesn't answer, and I feel like I've intruded on him and like I've insulted him.

"Can't you make a dinner at our place sometime this week?"

"What, Freddy?"

He wasn't paying attention. He was looking at a woman sitting three stools down from us. She's drinking bloody marys, and she's got two empties sitting next to her current drink. Garvin is not too swift about cleanup when his place is fairly crowded, as it is tonight.

"What are you looking at?"

"Nothing."

"You looking at her?"

He looks up at me now, as if to tell me 'piss off'.

"There's nothing wrong with looking at her, Stash. That's Karen Preszik. You know. She works at the lumberyard. She keeps the books."

"I thought I recognized her."

"You probably saw her on TV."

"TV? How?"

"Don't you watch wrestling?"

"Wrestling? Yeah, I—"

"She's a lady wrestler. She's a bad guy. When they come to Chicago, she wrestles the headliner, and she's the bad guy. But she always loses, of course."

"She's a wrestler?"

"Yeah. She goes under the name of Madonna Freedom. She wears a getup like that broad rock singer, Madonna. You know. But she's a little bit larger than her famous namesake, I think."

"Really? She doesn't look that big or bulky to me."

"She works in a lumber yard. I hear she totes some of the logs off the truck, when they arrive from Oregon."

"I don't think that's funny, Freddy. She looks kind of nice, as far as I can tell."

I can hear the sincerity in his voice, so I lay off. I take a look at Karen Preszik, and I'm thinking maybe Stash is right. She's not an unattractive woman, although she appears to have a slight pooch on her stomach when I see her in her one-piece bathing suit on TV. She calls them wrestling tights, I'm sure. But she's not fat, and she's not un-feminine.

Then it lights up, inside me.

"Why don't you ask her to join us for a drink?"

"I couldn't, Freddy. No. I don't think so."

"Why not?"

"I just couldn't, I don't think."

I don't press him any further. If I learned anything from my wife, Dee Dee, it's how dangerous it is to try and be a middle man for any budding romances. So I back off before I get my nose stung.

Then I open my mouth in spite of all those intelligent reasons to keep out of Stanley's business.

"How long has it been since you've been out with a lady?"

"What'd you say?"

He's still peeking at Karen. And then she looks down his way, and he jerks his face toward me. He's in a crimson flush.

"I said, when's the last time you were out with a bona fide lady?"

He takes a drink from his beer.

"I don't know. Don't go out much...Who wants a fat old man?"

"You're forty-two. What's old about forty-two?"

"I'm fat and I'm going bald."

"Stash, women dig bald, on men. You can always get rid of the fat."

"I've tried diet pills."

"I'm talking about exercise, Stashu. You don't do much of that, now do you?"

"I'm too tired when I get home from work."

"You're too tired because you're out of shape and overweight."

I immediately recognize the cruelty and stupidity of what I've just said. I put my hand on his forearm.

"I'm telling you you can do something about it. Marya was a pretty woman, wasn't she?"

His head snaps up with the mention of his ex-wife's name.

"Marya is beautiful. Still is."

"Right. And you must've been attractive to her if she married you and stayed with you all those years."

I'm at a dead end because I have no intention of reminding him about why she left him. He's already reminded himself often enough of the bum rap she threw at him as a reason to split.

"All I'm trying to say is you're no lost cause, Stanley. All you got to do is start working out with me a few nights a week and you'll look ten years younger. That's all I meant. You're a far piece away from over the hill. I can't stand to see you like this, Stash. Why'd you divorce me and Dee Dee and all your friends, along with your old lady?"

His eyes are leveled on mine. It seems we're locked onto each other for a very long moment.

Then he shifts his eyes down to Karen the Wrestler once more.

"Five years is a long time, Freddy. It's long enough."

Then he turns back to me, lifts his beer glass, and clinks his stein against mine.

His enthusiasm is at first a bit hard to take. When I finish my mile around the health club's track, Stanley's still going. If I run a mile, he has to run a mile and a half. If I do thirty pushups, he's got to do forty-five.

While he's trying to finish an extra set of stomach curls, I try to slow him down before he kills himself.

"This ain't a race, Stan. This ain't a competition."

"I know," he grunts.

It's hard to try to retard his progress. He's lost fifteen pounds in three weeks. It's not just from the workouts here at the club, either, I understand. He's told me the whole tale about his change in eating habits. He counts calories, he's cut off the sugar and starch, and he's lowered his cholesterol intake. No more beer or alcohol of any kind, and no more pizza.

The man has become a fanatic in just three quarters of a month. I had no idea of the monster I was creating at Garvin's, those short weeks ago.

"I feel great," Stanley grumbles, finishing his set of stomach curls. Curls are when you lift your legs, stiff, six inches off the floor and when you also raise your shoulder blades six inches off the carpet. You hold until you feel an excruciating pain in your abdomen. It works a lot better than situps because situps only settle your flab. And Stanley is working on a stomach that is as tight as it was when he was in high school and when he was in the Army with me.

When we were in Vietnam, we both weighed about 155 pounds. When we got out, I zoomed to nearly 200 and Stash bloated to 185. He's not tall enough or muscular enough to handle all that weight, so he says he'd like to get down to 165. He has only five more pounds to go.

And he does look like he's ten years younger. Even the thinning, receding hairline doesn't make him look forty-two any longer.

The health club membership was a gift from my wife, Dee. I've never belonged to one before, and Stash and I have never stepped inside a place like this previously.

What grabbed our immediate attention were the broads in the tights. Dee tells me some of these females spend a good half hour putting on makeup before they come out into the gym or track area. Imagine putting on a face to come out here and grunt and groan and exert yourself for an hour.

When Stanley and I emerge from the lockerroom we're both wearing our khaki gym shorts that we kept from our PT days in the Army, and we're wearing our 'Herd' t-shirts that we had made for us when we were stationed near Bong Son in 1969. The 183rd, the Herd. And I've got on high-topped black Converse All-Stars gym shoes, and Stan's wearing red K-Mart special high-tops as well.

We are noticed. But no one laughs at the two older men. Perhaps it's because they're too stunned. Maybe it's bad form to laugh at the peasants, I'm thinking. Whatever it is, I'm a little irritated at the snooty looks we're getting from the males and females around here.

"We've entered yuppie heaven, Freddy. Don't let them get to you."

Stan is still at his calisthenics. These gawkers haven't seemed to bother him these last three weeks, and perhaps it's because his results are more important to him than the attitude of these habitues of this yuppie clubhouse. I'm the one who's steamed about these rubberneckers. Stan remains unperturbed.

A blonde and a redhead, both very well-formed, trot by us on the track. They stop suddenly and walk over to us. Stash is still at his stomach curls and I'm sitting on the floor next to him.

"Is *The Herd* some kind of heavy metal group?" the redhead giggles. The blond is blushing and struggling not to explode.

"Yeah. Heavy metal," I tell her. "Real heavy metal. And heavy lead, too. You better get back to your laps before the recess bell rings," I tell the blonde and the redhead.

Their laughter dissolves. They've caught my drift.

"You don't have to be snotty," the blonde whines. "We were only tryin' to be friendly."

They turn and bolt back toward the track.

"You gotta loosen up, Freddy," Stash laughs. "You're tight as a virgin on her honeymoon. Ease up."

I'm the guy who's supposed to be helping him, I'm thinking, and Stanley's telling me to loosen up.

I think I'm getting real tired of life in the fast lane around here. I've lost ten pounds the last three weeks, just watching Stanley sweat.

Dee has been in charge of the last leg in the rejuvenation of Stanley Sliwa. She's looked around at her work —she's the manager of the Hinsdale Toys R Us store— and she thinks she's found the woman for Stanley.

Her name is January Juricka.

"January Juricka?" I ask Dee.

"She goes by Jan, once you get to know her."

"And you're going to have them come to dinner to meet each other?"

"I've described Stan to her. She says he sounds fine."

"And what does she—"

"She's very pretty. Thirty-two, and divorced. No kids."

I should be suspicious, but if I am I'll be doubting my wife's opinion. She knows Stan, and I know she'll try to do her best for him.

Stanley isn't very worried about his encounter with January Juricka. At Garv's, where we meet for a Diet Coke on this Thursday night, he appears to be at total ease with the idea of meeting up with a woman named after the coldest month of the year.

"I think it sounds like a very distinctive, elegant name."

He takes a slug out of his Diet Coke can. He's got me on this Nutra-sweet stuff now. No more beer for either of us, he says. We've worked too hard to go back to our old ways.

I'm so proud of him that I can't sneak a real drink in front of him. Even at home I've got a twelve pack of Old Style that's been gathering dust in our downstairs refrigerator. I haven't got the heart to imbibe behind his back. Stanley has us both weigh in every time we go to the health club. Although I was a bit put off by the people at that club, Stanley insisted we keep up our exercise routine.

After he belts down the Diet Coke, he says he wants me to take a ride with him. When I ask, he puts a warning finger to his lips.

We arrive at the Mages Sports Store.

As soon as we get inside, the salesman spots two easy marks. I think it was the eye contact come-on that Stanley provided as we entered the place.

"Yes, gentlemen?"

"Stanley?"

"We need some running gear," Stan informs him.

"Brand, sir? Anything you had in mind?"

"Stanley?"

"This is all on me, Freddy. You turned me on to running."

"Turned you on?"

"Yes. And now I'm going to put something back. I'm buying, and there ain't going to be any argument."

He is one stubborn Polski. I've known him since high school, and when he decides something, everyone around him had better learn to live with their fate.

"Let's have a look at the Nike."

"Yes, sir."

There was a gleeful smile on that salesman. I thought it might have even contained a dose of malevolence in it.

Stash grabs me by the arm and urges me onward.

It's the Thursday night before the big Friday night encounter for Stanley with January Juricka. He wants to lose three more pounds before he makes his big move back into the mainstream of dating and romance, he tells me.

We're outfitted in four hundred dollars' worth of sweats and gym shoes. Excuse me, they're called 'running shoes.' I insisted that I pay for my half of the goods, but Stanley demanded that the salesman at Mages put it all on his Visa card. I've got to think of a way to reimburse him, but with Stanley Sliwa, payback is nearly impossible. Generosity has always been one of his most glaring faults. He was always broke in Vietnam because he always loaned out all of his cash. And when R and R came, he stayed in the bush because he was too kindly and proud to ask those deadbeat bums to pay back what they owed him. He wouldn't borrow or take money from me, either. He is a very proud and stubborn man when he wants to be.

The redhead and the blonde are scooting around the track. When they come around the curve by Stanley and me (doing our

loosening and stretching), they don't even shoot a glance our way.
"Young skunks always hold grudges," Stan says.
"Maybe they like Adidas better," I tell him.
"What's this January Juricka look like?"
"I told you, Stan. Only Dee Dee knows that for sure. We'll just have to rely on her good taste."
"Dee wouldn't fix me up with a corpse."
"Of course not."
"She'd be looking out for my better interests."
"Certainly."
"She wouldn't lay anything lame on me."
"You know it."
He sits up.
"Do I really look any younger?"
"January's not exactly a chicken, herself."
"Ten years younger, though."
"Divorced, Stanley. She's not going to cry if you both wind up back at your place, in bed."
"I never went out with a woman who bedded down on the first date."
"You never dated a divorced woman. She hasn't got time to play Little Red Riding Hood."
"Meaning?"
"Meaning you play it by ear and you stop being so nervous about January Juricka. She's just as nervous about you. You've been married to a beautiful woman and you know everything you need to know about how to treat them. Now it's your turn to loosen up."
"I could use a beer."
"We'll have a few after."
"I won't lose my three pounds, then."
"She ain't going to bring a scale over to the house, Stash."
"But I'll know."
"So we'll drink a diet beer. Half the calories."
The blonde and the redhead circle the track once more. This time the redhead says something to her partner and they both smile at each other.
"I thought the Nike was sexier than the Adidas, Freddy. Didn't you?"

*

My wife is a sweet woman. I love her dearly. She means well, and she has almost everyone's best interests at heart.

However.

January Juricka walks through our front door and the first thing I notice as I shake her hand is her black nail polish. Her lipstick is just this side of darkness, as well, but there's a red tinge to it when the light of our living room strikes it just right.

Stanley is speechless when he sees her. Her hair is not quite in that old-styled buoffant, but it is flipped over to the right side of her head. Very fashionable, I suppose. Very with-it.

"Hello," Stanley pronounces as he takes January's hand.

Maybe I am overreacting, because Stanley seems to have something in his eye for her. At least he doesn't run out of the room calling me a double-dealing traitor. But Stash would never make a scene, I know.

He would endure.

We all four sit down in our living room. Our adopted son has been put to bed early so that we could have a quiet dinner together. And later Stan is supposed to take January down to Rush Street.

Maybe this is her Rush Street getup. Maybe when she goes home after all this, she turns into a mousey housewife-type.

She looks like that writer broad who's so hot right now in New York. I saw a picture of her and I read a story about her in the *Tribune Sunday Section* on Books. Tama or Tamara or somebody. She wrote something about some slaves of New York, I think it was.

And when I think of Stanley Sliwa with January Juricka at Rush Street on some disco floor, I have to truly control myself.

Then it shames me to think of how ridiculous Stan's going to look with this woman. She's white collar and he's blue collar. Even though I finally took a degree in college, I think of myself as working class. Ever since I worked summers at the old man's chemical plant, where Stan still works, I think of myself as part of the working class. It's hard to toss off that association. Maybe I don't really want to throw off the old ties, either.

I'm trying to think of some way of working Stanley away from Rush Street, and away from this Tama Whatsername Lookalike.

Then it strikes me as presumptuous of me to pre-see what's going to take place between them tonight.

Maybe they'll fall in love. Maybe she'll wash off her black nail polish. Maybe underneath all that mousse there's real hair.

And maybe I'm pre-judging what's going to turn out to be a fantastic female.

"I've got two tickets to the Whitney Houston concert at the Horizon tomorrow night. I was wondering if you'd like to go, Stan," January lays it on him as soon as we're seated on our two living room couches. She and Stan are sitting next to each other, just as Dee Dee has orchestrated it.

"Sure. Who's Whitney Houston?"

Dee and January laugh in good humor, but Stanley and I are lost by their hale mirth.

"Whitney, Whitney Houston. The pop singer. You know. The black girl. Very pretty."

Dee smiles nervously.

"I don't listen to much rock on the radio stations. I used to like The Temptations and The Four Tops, back when I was in the Army."

Stanley is treading water, I can tell. He's no big music fan. He used to listen to the opera over the Armed Forces Station, when they weren't playing Jimi Hendrix or The Doors. He was the only opera fan in the platoon, and his affection for that heavy caterwallering was something he took a lot of heat for.

"It's O.K. if you don't go for her kind of music."

"No. I'd really love to go with you. I think it would be very interesting to see her. Now that you say her name again, it seems to me I have seen her on TV in one of those rock videos."

Stanley's full of caca. He never watches MTV. Why? Because he has no cable at his house.

"Ohhh."

Dee is still in her stunned silence. Even she is aware of the disaster the two of us have wrought on top of Stanley Sliwa.

Again I tell myself that I'm overdoing the disaster scenario. Stanley could be getting the best time of his life tonight, and tomorrow night for all I know. You can't always predict the Stash. He fools you. He's not always the conservative, down-the-middle-of-the-road Polack that I'd like to think he is.

He married Marya, afterall.

I think that Marya and January would get along fine. They could talk about Greenwich Village and the Bay Area and sushi and the San Francisco poets of the 1960's, and they'd probably hit it off like sisters.

Maybe Stan sees that offbeat thing in January Juricka. Perhaps I'd better shut off my prognosticator and see how things in fact do go. Come on, January, surprise us all. Be the woman that Stanley's been looking for for five years. Replace the original. Fill up my best friend's heart again. Come on. Lacquered nails and all, come on.

"I hear you two guys were together in Vietnam."

"They were. Together," Dee manages to add. Her first conversational offering. I feel like kicking her in the shin. So I glare at her, instead. I have the feeling she's about ready to stick her tongue out at me.

"We were stationed in a place called Bong Son. It's near the coast," Stan tells her.

"Did you see *Platoon?* I saw it. It was disgusting. But I read it was really realistic. I was a little kid when most of that stuff was going on. So I really can't say I know much about it."

Stan looks at me for help. I feel like raising my palms toward him, but I hold back.

"No. I haven't seen it. But I liked *The Deerhunter.* I thought the wedding scene was great," Stan tells her.

"I saw it on cassette. I thought it was too depressing, with the Russian roulette."

"Let's get away from the war," I hear myself saying.

"Yeah," January says. "Let's get away from all that heavy stuff."

She smiles, and her teeth are porcelain and perfect. I'll bet she never had a cavity. She's been on fluoride all her life.

"I was happy as hell to get away from it," Stan smiles.

"Time to eat," Dee breathes out, relievedly, as the timer bell goes off from the kitchen.

We all rise and head toward the next room, the dining room. We have a large house, now that we've moved to the suburb of Hinsdale. Stash told me he couldn't believe I could ever be comfortable in a neighborhood where your neighbors are hundreds of feet away from you. He can't understand a block where all the neighbors can't sit out on their tiny porches and hold a totally audible conversation with five or six of their immediate neighbors.

Hinsdale is not like the old neighborhood, Stash has reminded me more than once.

Dee made a bottom round roast beef for us. My favorite roast. We sit down while she goes to bring in the food.

When the beef arrives January shrivels her nose up just slightly.

"Dee, I don't want to offend you, but I won't be able to eat any of that beef."

"Why's that?" Dee queries politely.

"I'm a vegetarian...I thought you knew. I'm sorry."

"That's, that's O.K. We've got plenty of vegetables and a big salad. Will that do?"

"Oh, sure. I just didn't want you to think I was being a pain by not eating the meat. I guess I should have told you."

"That's just more for us," I say, and I feel as stupid as the statement the moment it leaves my lips.

January tries to smile but succeeds in a slight blush that accentuates her nearly-black lipstick. Dee glares at me with venom, and Stash is turning very pale.

"Hey, Dee's made two green vegetables and corn, too, and like she said, we're big on salads in this house," I try to apologize.

"It'll be fine. Everything smells wonderful," she says to Dee.

My wife is the consummate pragmatist. She can adapt to anything. If she were a dinosaur a million years ago, she would've found some new shrubbery to sustain her life. She's a survivor, I'm saying. So, almost unruffled, she serves the dinner.

Stanley and January and Dee and I finish our meal in twenty minutes.

In almost complete silence.

Toward the end of the meal January says, "I can't believe all the trouble you went to to put out this gorgeous dinner."

There is a disconcerting sincerity in what she says and how she says it. And now I try to look past her cosmetics.

She's in her early thirties. Past her dating prime, or will be shortly. Her prospects for finding another man are dwindling as this decade progresses. Where will she meet men? By being fixed up, like tonight? Will she go to bars and bistros and discos? And who will she encounter in those places? Men who go to bars and bistros and discos.

I look at January, and then I look at Stan, and my heart wants to crumble and disintegrate. I want to embrace them both.

But I know I can't help either of them. They weren't made for each other, Christ knows, but just this once I wish it had all been different and that they'd taken one look into each other's eyes and had fallen madly into a state of bliss for one another.

Dee says I'm the romantic in the family. I don't think of myself as an idealist, but maybe she's got something there.

I take one last, sad look at the two of them and suddenly I want to cry for them both.

But Dee brings in the chocolate cake she's made especially for the occasion, and my sympathy is diverted.

"What's the matter, Freddy? When are you coming to bed?"

She's in her nightgown, the thin, flimsy one that she knows drives me mad. She's standing in the darkened hallway, and I can only just make out her lean outline.

It's 1:30 A.M.

"I'll be right in."

Her form disappears now, into our bedroom.

I feel like I should call Stanley at his place and make him report on what happened at Rush Street. The reason I want to know is so that I can throw in my apology for getting him involved in a blind date. Not because January Juricka was a dog, because she was not. She was an attractive woman and, I suppose, a very fashionable lady. I want to apologize for sticking my nose into his love life, as though I were someone who had the ability to make happiness come his way.

Dee doesn't seem to feel too badly about the evening, however. She seemed to just shrug it off as if it were simply one of those life things where it simply doesn't work out the way you'd hoped it would, but there's no harm done.

That's what I'm wondering. If there's any harm done. I have a feeling there aren't any mean bones in January's body, but Stash could have suffered through one of the most uncomfortable nights of his life because of me. That's why I can't go to bed yet.

I should call him and see what happened. So I pick up the phone in the living room and I dial his phone.

Maybe he got as unlucky as I think he did and he went to Garvin's to close the place down.

So I call the Comeback, but Stanley's not there. Hasn't been there, either.

"Freddy," her voice comes wafting out of the bedroom. "You get away from that phone and stop worrying about him. He's a big boy. Get in here. I'm lonely."

I put the receiver down before I get the notion to call the cops and report a missing person.

Maybe they ran off to Vegas and got—

"Freddy! Get in here. The sheets are cold."

I remember she's wearing that see-through nightgown. I picture the doe-like quality of my wife's light tan flesh.

"You're on your own, Stan," I tell the receiver, as I put it gently back in its cradle.

Five days go by and no word from Stanley. I call his place, but every time there's no answer. I don't want to call him at work because that tends to frighten guys at the plant. They think someone's hurt or sick at home if they get calls there.

On another Thursday night at Garvin's Comeback Inn, after a heartbreaking 6-5 loss to the Dewdrop Inn Jesters, Stanley Sliwa comes loping into the bar. It's 9:00 P.M. again, and I again know what time Stanley has arrived because the Cub game is once again being televised from the West Coast. This time they're in L.A.

"I've been trying to get a hold of you for a week. Where've you been?"

"I thought I'd see you at the health club. Where've you been?"

Stash bought himself a membership the second week we were into our routine of workouts. He said he didn't want to leech off my membership for the rest of his life.

"I've been busy with summer league baseball. You know, for the high school."

"I lost two more pounds. Might make it down to—"

"You know what I want to know,"

"No, no. She was a nice lady. Nothing wrong with that number at all."

"Then why the sour look?"

"You know why."

"Because she didn't bring joy into your life."

"No. We just didn't do what you hoped we would do. Lecher! Pervert!"

He smiles at me to try to tell me to back off.

"I didn't want to know the gory details, Stash."

"That'd be a first for you, Freddy."

"No. I mean it. I was hoping something good might have happened."

"I hated Whitney Houston. But I didn't tell her. And she knew it anyway. We stayed out late both nights—"

"I tried to call you."

"What the hell for?"

"To see how it went."

"Thanks, Dad, but no thanks. My old man's still alive in Florida. He never calls me to find out how it went. Anyway, we went dancing after your place, and I made a complete jackass out of myself. Only thing that saved me was it was so crowded at Mother's that no one even noticed what an ortho I was, on the floor."

"She a good dancer?"

"Of course. That's what made me look even worse, to anyone with eyes."

"Good moves, huh?"

"She's an attractive woman."

"Hell, get to the good stuff."

"I thought you didn't want to know the bloody stuff."

I raise my eyebrows at him.

"Tough stuff, Alfred, because there are no gory details to pass on."

"You didn't even try?"

"We're friends, I think. She wants to go to the opera with me."

"And that's all?"

"That's it, Fredo."

He orders us two Diet Cokes, even though he sees the beer sitting in front of me.

"You're off your regimen."

"Yeah. I thought you'd quit now, too. Go back to the way we used to."

"Not me, pal."

"Still have aspirations of chasing down some young thing?"

"As a matter of fact, Freddy, that's why I'm here tonight."

"You made a connection of your own?"

"You might say."

"Where'd you meet?"

"Right about where we're sitting at this very moment. But hang on a minute. I just wanted to thank you and Dee for the whole setup. It was kind. I mean it."

"Jesus, don't water-up on me now."

"I won't. I swear I won't."

"I just wish it had been different between you and that January."

"She ain't me and she ain't us, Freddy. But I don't hold it against her. Hell, she's ten years younger than we are. She comes from a different world. She'll wind up with some yuppie-lawyer type. Somebody freshly divorced, like her. Don't worry about January Juricka. You look past the hair and the nails and the Whitney Houston concerts, you've got a decent lady."

"The strange thing about you, Stanley, is that you never have anything rotten to report about people. What the hell's the matter with you?"

"I don't know, Freddy. I guess I'm just not a student of human nature, like you."

He grips my forearm strongly, on top of the bar, and then he lets go when Garvin approaches with our Diet Cokes.

"You two turnin' into a couple of fairies? Am I interruptin' somethin' private?" Garvin sasses.

Then he walks away with my five dollar bill. I always wonder if he's coming back with my change.

Shockingly, there's a forearm around Stash's throat.

"What the—"

"Karen," Stash gurgles.

She releases her hold on his throat, and she sits down between us as I move one over.

It's Karen Preszik. Madonna Freedom to those fans who love to hate her.

"Freddy, this is Karen."

"Hi," she shakes my hand strongly, in a terrifyingly masculine grip.

"This is that connection I made that I was telling you about. In this very spot, where we sit and talk right now."

"Stash is coming to my bout tonight at the Rosemont. It's for the women's championship. Want to come with us and see me lose? Only you can't tell anyone the outcome, O.K.? It's part of the theater, you know?"

I think my mouth's hanging open, so I close it.

"Hell of a bout, Freddy. It's going to take thirty minutes for Madonna Freedom to succumb to Maryann Flasher. Come on with us. Listen to that. Ah, the juker. It ain't Wagner, but it'll do. Do you think I might have this dance before we make your 10:30 date with destiny?" he asks Karen.

"Sure, but just one dance. Then we gotta leave."

Some old guy, a WWII vet, put his quarter in and played Sinatra and Bennett.

It's playing "I Left My Heart in San Francisco," right now.

Karen gets up and walks toward the small rectangle of tile that is Garvin's version of a dance floor. I notice what a pretty woman she is, now that I've seen her closeup.

Stash bends toward me before he joins his date for the evening.

"You gotta do for yourself when it come to these affairs of the heart. And you know what, Freddy?"

"No. What?"

"We went to high school with Karen. She's just two years younger than we are. She's from our old neighborhood."

"Is she?"

"Don't be surprised if I'm engaged by the end of the weekend."

"Come on, Stan."

"Who knows? We've got that secret rhythm. I knew it the first time I talked to her. Hell, Freddy. She's one of us!''

He laughs, darts toward Karen, and he takes her into a grip which is more likely suited for her squared circle than for a dance floor.

Maybe it's the romantic in me, like Dee says. But I don't see it as a 'hold' he's got her in. She's big enough to whip his ass anyway.

No, it's an embrace he's got her in, and it isn't a simple two-step he's leading her with.

It's a waltz.

And it isn't Tony Bennett singing about where he forgot a major organ, anymore. It's Strauss, and it's the Blue Danube, and I swear I can smell freshly cut flowers.

Maybe it's Garvin's Aqua Velva aftershave.

But the old World War II vet who stuffed the juker with the quarter's worth of music they're dancing to comes across the floor to Stash and Karen.

He hands Karen a white carnation. I can see it all clearly. They stop dancing for a moment, and she finds something to pin the carnation to her blouse.

Stash plants a long and passionate buss on her and everyone in this crazy bar is suddenly applauding, me included. Then it becomes even rowdier as the post-softball game crowd begins to cheer until they become hoarse. Everyone's laughing and clapping and hooting and hollering.

And then, when Stanley Sliwa takes Karen Preszik into his arms once more to finish his dance, it becomes quiet enough that we can all hear every word of Tony Bennett's lyrics.

Something is happening inside me as I watch my friend whirl round and round. I have an electric impression that just as quickly as I think of it, it fades away.

I'm trying to remember that evasive thought, but I cannot, as Stanley moves Karen around and around Garvin's dance floor.

Stash bends toward her and kisses her carnation and the crowd erupts again.

Then we are quiet again as we watch him lead her across the floor, in perfect step together, in perfect communion with the music coming from Garvin's aging Wurlitzer.